MW00876288

THE SICKNESS: A PSYCHOLOGICAL THRILLER

BRITNEY KING

COPYRIGHT

Hot Banana Press

Cover Design by Britney King LLC

Cover Image by Robert Thiem

Copy Editing by Librum Artis

Proofread by Proofreading by the Page

First Edition: 2023

ISBN 13: 9798391664543

ISBN 10: 8391664543

britneyking.com

"The road to hell is paved with good intentions."

— Proverb

THE SICKNESS

BRITNEY KING

PROLOGUE

The world is spinning too fast for me to make any sense of it. Fear and desperation choke the air as a steady buzz of panicked whispers fill the background like static. The wind whips my hair across my face as I stand on the deck, the ocean crashing beneath me. A thousand eyes seem to be upon me.

My fellow passengers are in chaos, their faces wild and terror-stricken as they grab supplies and flee from the horror. The ship isn't as full as it once was, but it's still crowded, and people race in all directions, panic spreading like wildfire. Everywhere I look, people are in a state of desperation. Some run, some cower, and some simply stand frozen, as if waiting for the inevitable.

I search for Dad, and I feel my own panic rise within me. I see hundreds of faces, but none are his.

Then I hear him calling out my name.

"Abby!"

"Dad?"

"Abby!"

Finally, I spot him across the deck, arms full of water bottles, and I exhale the breath I'd been holding. He motions for me to move forward as planned, and I dash toward the bread line, thirst scratching at my throat after a full day without water. Over my shoulder, I watch my dad weave through the crowd. He has that same look on his face he had when he told me about this trip—determination mixed with dread—and I know what's going through his head: We should have never gotten on this ship.

Roger Atkins has never been a cruise ship kind of guy, but considering the circumstance, what could he say?

"It'll be an adventure, I guess," he'd finally said, and he was right.

"Next!" a woman shouts, and I move forward in line.

I hand over my ration card to a lady with dead eyes. Children aren't supposed to be on deck when rations are dispersed, but I'm not most children. I'm sixteen, though I might as well be eighty. People frequently utter words like "last resort" and "little hope" when they think I'm not listening. One look at me and it goes without saying.

I grab two loaves of bread and can't help the satisfied grin that washes over my face. We have water and we have bread. Everything is right in the world again. I glance toward my dad in triumph, but something else captures my eye.

An eerie stillness has draped the deck like a blanket, and an icy chill runs down my spine.

A man is wielding a gun. He's pointing it straight at the crowd. My heart stops, and my breath catches in my throat.

I scan the deck, but Dad is not where I last saw him. I don't see him anywhere. Fear courses through me like icy nails, freezing me in place. I know I should run, but where? A single gunshot slices through the air—I scream in sheer terror.

I am not the only one.

Everything happens so fast. I don't have time to run. I don't even have time to think. One shot evolves into many. Bullets whip through the air in all directions. The man turns and aims at me and instinctively, I hit the deck. My vision blurs, but not before I see drops of my blood splatter around me. Liquid heat blankets my skin and searing pain rips through my stomach. Then everything goes dark.

When I stir back to consciousness, the air is ringing with sirens and frantic screams. Burning pain radiates through my chest with every breath, and my pulse races, a reminder I'm still alive.

One thought thunders in my head: *find Dad.*

I push onto my elbows and survey the carnage around me. Bodies are strewn across the deck like broken dolls, some silent and still, others writhing in pain as fellow passengers scavenge their rations. The wood beneath them is drenched in blood, a river of red that covers the world in crimson.

I close my eyes for a moment and will the darkness to take me. I don't want to die like this, but I don't want to live this way either.

Someone tugs at the loaves of bread that I have gripped firmly, and my eyes snap open. A wild-eyed woman pries at my fingers, but I refuse to let go. "I have children."

"I am a child," I bellow, clutching the bread to my chest. The woman turns and walks away without a word. Just once she looks back, for what I don't know—I assume to see if I'm dead yet.

I give her the finger. That's when I see him wading through the sea of people, shouting my name. He doesn't stop until he's reached me. Relief is evident in his eyes, but they widen when he sees the scarlet stains on my shirt.

Dad pulls me into his arms and whispers words of comfort. For a moment, all I feel is relief—relief that we are both alive.

He looks into my eyes and smiles softly, "Abby, it'll be all right."

"My stomach—"

He reaches down and peels the blood-soaked shirt away from my skin. "It's not that bad," he says, after exhaling a heavy breath. "You're gonna be fine."

I nod. And stupidly, I believe him.

1

Roger

Eleven days earlier

I clench my daughter's hand with a death-like grip as we enter the terminal. The weight of dread sits like a boulder on my chest, an ever-present reminder of my raging hatred of the ocean. And boats, I'm not a fan of those either, even though Abby has warned me about referring to it as such.

"It's a ship!" she hisses. "How many times do I have to tell you?"

I shrug. "Semantics."

"Please," she says. "For once, just be happy."

"I am happy."

"Well, you don't look it."

I force a wide grin, baring my teeth. "There. How's that?"

"God! You're impossible."

I can't argue with that, so I vow to try harder. My daughter's dream is about to be fulfilled, and the only thing I can think of is that if I don't tamper my anxiety, I am going to break her heart. Again. I have done all I can to prepare, but I still feel overcome with the feeling that this trip is a terrible idea. And now that we're here, I am reminded why. Our lives demand order and calm. Schedules and routine. This place is a zoo.

Not only that, but we couldn't be more out of place. These people do not look like us. They don't speak like us. They are not what you would consider even remotely near our income bracket. I don't want to be a charity case. I do not want my daughter to be a charity case. And yet, I realize this trip is bigger than that. It means a lot to Abby, probably more than anything ever has. I tried to convince her she should choose somewhere else—*anywhere* else, but no dice. My sister says beggars can't be choosers, but I don't see it that way.

"Is it me or is it stuffy in here?"

Abby gives me a sideways glance. "It's you."

I have the sudden urge to step out of line, to say thanks, but no thanks. I've seen enough. I have zero interest in pretending I'm someone or *something* I'm not. Not for a week, not for a day, not even for as long as it takes to get through this line. But then Abby looks up at me with a hopeful smile, and I forget the logic in my thoughts.

"Come on, Roger. At least *try* to pretend like you want to be here..."

It has never been more obvious that my daughter and I come from different generations. "Just because they can afford this," I say, "doesn't make them better than us. And what did I tell you about calling me Roger?"

"No one said anything about anyone being better than anyone else, *Father*."

I point out the length of the line. I guess even rich people have to wait occasionally. "Why don't we go grab a bite to eat? We can come back when the crowd thins out."

"It's not that long," Abby counters. "You go. I'll hold our place."

My daughter knows better. She knows I won't leave her, and she knows the point was to get *her* away from the crowd. "Never mind," I grumble. "But just so you know, this isn't my idea of fun."

"Believe me, I know."

"What do you say we stay here in Miami? We could hang out on the beach—"

"No."

"Fine." I hadn't thought she'd change her mind in the five minutes since I'd last posed the question, but it was worth a shot. "Did I mention I hate boats?"

Clearly, I am the only one who feels this way. Passengers everywhere chatter with excitement, except for the group of people kneeling in a tight circle, their hands clasped, murmuring words in unison.

"What are they doing?" Abby asks, her voice low with curiosity.

"No idea," I say. "Praying, it looks like."

She raises an eyebrow. "Weird."

"Yeah," I reply. "Hey, as soon as we get through this line, let's go check out the cabin."

My daughter narrows her eyes at me. "I want to look around first."

"Cabin first, then we look around," I say firmly.

She rolls her eyes, and I'm glad there's still a bit of the sixteen-year-old left in my daughter yet. "If you say so," she huffs.

"I say so."

"You worry too much."

"For good reason," I tell her. "Who else is going to?"

But she's right. Despite all the reassurances I've been given, I'm terrified our bags won't make it to the cabin. I need to see for myself that they have. Before we disembark.

My daughter needs the medical supplies in that luggage. Her life depends on it, and regardless of my pleas, the crew would only allow one carry-on. They didn't come right out and say it, but it wouldn't be a good look, me handling my own bags, considering the demographic they cater to.

"We take care of everything," they said. "Every last detail—you leave it to us."

The line snakes around, and as we edge closer to the ship, my mouth drops. Talk about detail. Its grand hull is decorated with a vibrant mural, and its dark windows glimmer in the late afternoon sun. A refreshing breeze carries salty air, and streamers dance playfully like ribbons in a parade.

With a brow cocked, Abby motions toward the upper deck. The crew is abuzz with activity, hustling to make sure everything is ready for our voyage. Many of them are literally running back and forth across the ship. With a nudge, she points out that I should feel bad for thinking them inept.

"About the worrying," she says, "I wish you'd give it a rest. Otherwise we might as well have stayed at home."

I stand frozen in the security line, my gaze locked with my daughter's. We both know the risks that come with this trip, yet there's a steely determination in her eyes. I pull her close, wrapping my arms around her petite frame. She wriggles in protest, but I refuse to let go. She's my only child, and I'm never going to let anything bad happen to her. "You're right," I say. "The worrying, it stops now."

"Doubt it."

"You'll see," I tell her and leave it at that. I'm glad Abby is feeling more herself today, but one can only take so much teenage banter. We move through security and then onward to the window where our cruise cards will be issued. The line is long, and I'm concerned she needs to sit down. She's been well these past few weeks, but things can change on a dime.

"I'm fine," she says, reading my mind.

"I know."

We inch forward, and there's some sort of commotion ahead. People press together and crane their necks to see what's happening. The crowd parts as everyone looks to see what all the yelling is about. I move to the center and can't believe my eyes.

2

Roger

A group of sunburned, highly inebriated men have a woman surrounded. They circle her like vultures. At first I think it's some kind of entertainment put on by the cruise line, but I soon understand what's actually happening.

The men are incessant with their catcalling. When they begin pawing at the woman's skirt, she strikes one of them across the face. "I said don't touch me!"

The man cries out, clapping a hand over his nose. "You dumb bitch! You made me bleed!"

His friends check him over, and riotous laughter erupts. But the woman's slap only serves to incite the men even more. They turn on her with a vengeance. I glance around to see if anyone in line is going to come to her rescue, but no one moves.

I search for a crew member, someone in uniform, security to defuse the situation. But the only crew I see are across the terminal.

"Get your hands off me!" the woman shouts.

They don't listen, and they don't stop. The taunting only grows louder and crueler.

"Boys will be boys," a woman behind me says to the man standing next to her. "Looks like a bachelor party. Hopefully, they won't be too rowdy."

"Best we mind our own business," the man replies. "You see what she's wearing? She's asking for it."

I scan the terminal. The people off to the side are still chanting. The crew members are still nowhere in sight. The line creeps forward. One would think the security on these ships would be pretty tight, but I've watched my fair share of documentaries, and I know better.

"Wait here," I say to Abby.

"Dad, no—" She takes a hold of my shoulder. "We shouldn't get involved."

"We already are," I say loosening her grip. "Besides, who else is going to?"

"I don't know—security?"

"I don't see security. Do you?"

Abby pushes up on her tippy-toes. She scans the terminal. "I see a few of them by the entrance."

"Stay here," I say and then I push through the line, dashing over to where the group of men circle the woman. She was attractive from the back of the line, but she's even prettier up close. "There you are, honey," I say, lightly touching the small of her back, nudging her forward. "We're just over here."

The woman glares at me with a mixture of surprise, annoyance, and perhaps, finally, a hint of amusement. "Thanks, love," she says, patting my chest. "But I don't need you to come and save me. Look—I made him bleed."

I look from her to the group of drunks who are standing around her, now with their hands on their hips, equally curious and disappointed.

"Who the fuck are you?" the man with the bloody nose demands. He steps forward, cupping his face, his blood dripping through his knuckles.

"I'm—"

My mouth is half-open when Abby splits through the crowd. "Dad!" she says with relief. She turns to the woman. "Mom!" She wraps her arms around the lady's waist. "I've been looking everywhere for you!"

"Look at her kid," the guy says matter-of-factly. "She's sick. Man, y'all oughta be ashamed."

Laughter ripples through them. But not the woman, Abby, or I —we just stand there looking at each other.

Finally, a crew member arrives along with a lady in a Hawaiian shirt wearing leis around her neck. She points at the men. "It's them! These degenerates are harassing that poor woman!"

"What'd you call me?" the man with the bloody nose snarls. He lunges at the lady. I step in between the two of them and hold my hands up toward his chest. "Easy," I say.

He steps back on his heel and balls his fists. I shield my face and brace for impact. But then his friend tackles him from behind. "You heard the man, Chuck! He said take it easy."

I watch as both men tumble to the floor and tussle about. *Everyone* watches. Another man from their group tries to step in, but he gets dragged down too. The three of them wrestle like a pack of wild dogs.

The crew member nervously clicks her radio to call for help. A grim hush falls over the terminal. All eyes turn to the far corner, where a man writhes on the floor, contorting in pain. His agonized howls pierce the air. There is a collective gasp—even the men grappling at my feet pause in horror.

"Looks like a seizure," a lady behind me says. "But who knows? Nothing is ever as it seems. They let all kinds of riffraff on cruises nowadays..."

Her companion nods. "Yeah. Believe nothing you hear, and only half of what you see, right?"

It's chaos everywhere you look. Hundreds of people trying to board, a medical emergency, and a group of drunks harassing a woman. I can't say it's what I expected, but it's exactly what I expected. I can't wait to throw it in my sister's face.

"Get off me, Dan!" the guy with the bloody nose shouts.

"Say the magic word, Chucky-boy."

"Fuck off!"

More laughter ensues until eventually the men extract themselves from the dog pile they've created. Chuck staggers to his knees and turns all of his drunken fury my way. I widen my stance. I've seen that look before, and I know this guy's just getting warmed up.

His buddies help him to his feet. He straightens his shirt and then brushes himself off. Then he turns to me, his face set. "You better watch yourself," he hisses through gritted teeth.

"I didn't mean any harm."

"Yeah?" He stabs a finger into my chest. "Well, if I see your face again, I will fucking gut you."

I step back. "I don't doubt that."

Abby tugs on my sleeve. "Come on, Dad. He's just drunk."

The man glares at her. "I don't care what your deal is, little girl," he sneers. "I'll take that oxygen tank and shove it right up your ass."

I square my shoulders. "That's my daughter—"

"I don't give a damn who she is," he says, cutting me off. "If she gives me any more lip, I'll fucking gut her, too."

3

Passenger 327

I emerge from the shadows of the dock, my suitcase in one hand and a hammering heart in the other. With only a half hour to spare, I almost didn't make it. What a pity that would have been.

The salty air clings to my skin, and the sky is a deep, burning red. God, I love the ocean. There's so much promise in its depths. It feels good to be back.

An eerie silence drapes the harbor, broken only by the occasional creak of wooden planks and the incessant caw of seagulls.

When I get onto the ship, a hit of white-hot anticipation runs through me. I can't help but be awed by the sight of the grand cruise liner, with its gleaming exterior and multiple decks. They're all lined with luxurious amenities such as outdoor pools, hot tubs, and lounges. There is a magnificence to the ship that is not surprising, considering the price tag for the experience. An air of grandeur hangs over every corner of the vessel, and I wouldn't have it any other way.

The clientele that frequents the Grand Pacifica is an exclusive crowd, to be sure. The tinted windows gleam, and the deck is well polished, with the finest furniture and fixtures.

My heart races as I look up at the director, an imposing figure silhouetted against the fiery sky.

His voice booms across the deck. He means to sound cheery, but I can hear the air of foreboding as he says: "Welcome aboard!"

I look up to see him standing at the bow, a smirk and a menacing glint in his eyes. He seems to laugh at everyone—as if he knows their darkest secrets and is daring them to take this voyage, anyway.

Oh, wait. Never mind. That's me. How stupid these people are. They have no idea what's in store for them.

"For the next seven days," the director booms, "you will embark on a magical and wondrous journey. We will traverse the seas, explore new lands, and discover secrets that lie beyond the horizon. Are you ready for such an adventure?"

The passengers cheer in response. What a joke. Once again, I am reminded that *wealthy* doesn't mean *intelligent.* Quite the opposite, I assure you. The thing about rich people is that they must be wowed. They'll do a lot of stupid things in search of something new, something *different.*

This director seems to understand this quite well. He knows he must offer these people the idea of something they've never experienced before and may never experience again. So dramatic the wealthy are.

My heart flutters with excitement, but I also feel a sense of trepidation. I know that this grand cruise liner will bring me closer to the inevitable, to accomplishing what I set out to do, but I am wary of what I have to deal with in the meantime. People like this, being one.

The ship's whistle blows, signaling the start of the journey.

Soon, the vessel will drift away from the dock and out to sea. I can't wait to stand on deck watching as the coastline slowly disappears in the distance, pondering which of these losers I can pick off first.

The boat rocks rhythmically, and I instantly forget about the nightmarish darkness and concentrate on the task at hand. The open waters fill me with a sense of optimism, and even though I'm surrounded by almost eight hundred idiots, I know anything is possible.

A sensation of liberty washes over me, as if I'm truly alive for the first time in my life. I realize it's been too long since I've felt this way.

Sounds of music drift down from the upper deck and break my trance. I'm not familiar with the song, but I'm not surprised given the garbage modern bands churn out these days.

I climb the stairs and spot a stunning young woman in the corner chair, her journal open in her lap. I watch her write. She stops and looks out at the sea, but never at me. By the time I reach the bottom step, she's already turned her attention to her phone, her voice ringing out over the dreadful music.

I stop and listen. It's usually a person's voice that is often the first thing that leads me to kill them. How else can I explain it? It's an inner knowing.

At first, her voice makes me feel nothing. Then she huffs and jams her pen between the pages of her notebook, and slams it shut. I watch her as she gazes out into the distance, and I appreciate the fire in her eyes. She's younger than I thought, no older than midtwenties, with brown hair and big, round eyes. Carmel colored, I assume, but I can't wait to find out for sure.

I hear her murmur something about "charges" and "someone breathing down her neck." She sounds worried and desperate, exactly what I want.

She says, "I'm sorry I couldn't stay. They started asking too many questions... You know how it is... The charges? No, they dropped them… yeah, but they're still breathing down my neck… I'm thinking of disappearing for a while… Would it really be so bad?"

It's not so much what she says, but what she doesn't say.

She falls silent as the person on the other end of the line rattles on.

After an eternity, she finally speaks again. She's concerned about something—or *someone*—back home.

Finally, she whispers a soft goodbye. Then she stares out at the horizon for a long while before turning her attention back to the notebook in her lap. She starts to write—this time with more conviction than before, as if determined to exorcise some demon. That's when I realize we have more in common than I thought.

4

Roger

As I push the door to our cabin open, a wave of relief washes over me. My eyes take in the incredible interior—a sumptuous sofa, beds lined with goose-down pillows, mahogany tables carved with intricate designs—plus everything I requested to make this week comfortable for Abby.

Glancing over my shoulder, I see two security guards standing at the entrance to the hallway. After the altercation in the terminal, we were given a personal escort to our cabin, along with welcome drinks. An icy glass of whiskey for me and a Shirley Temple with a maraschino cherry for Abby.

I wouldn't have thought the drunkards would have been allowed to board, but I guess money talks. That and the young woman refused to speak up when questioned about the incident. After everything, she told the crew it was nothing. Just a simple "misunderstanding."

"Wow!" Abby gasps, eyes wide with admiration. "This is amazing."

"It's not bad."

"Are you feeling okay?" She gives me a onceover. "You're not seasick already, are you?"

I chuckle and ruffle her hair. "It's my job to do the worrying, remember?"

"Don't let those guys get to you, Dad."

"What guys?" I ask playfully. The truth is, my daughter is right. Those men from the terminal have gotten to me more than I care to admit. To think I'm trapped on a boat with them for a week only adds fuel to the anxiety I already have about this trip. Although it's a large ship, it's not actually *that* large—by cruise ship standards, it's considered a medium-sized vessel.

I feel the lurch and shudder beneath my feet; a signal that our departure is imminent. "Well, I guess there's no backing out now. It's just you and me, kid."

"And like a thousand other people."

"Same difference."

I walk over to the small refrigerator, fling it open, and survey the assortment of tiny bottles. The whiskey did nothing to take the edge off. "You promised," Abby says.

I pull out a water bottle and twist off the cap. "Promised what?"

"Nothing."

"I'm going to check out the bathroom," I say. "Need to get in there before I do?"

"Nope."

I catch my reflection in the bathroom mirror, and my chest tightens. I grip the vanity and stare into the mirror, trying to fight off the rising panic. Cold sweat streams down my face, and my breath comes in shallow bursts. To calm myself, I splash cold water on my face and wet down my hair. *I need a drink.* Promise or no promise. If I'm going to survive this trip, I'm going to need another drink. Once I get Abby's supplies and equipment unpacked, I'll steal a moment for myself.

I use the toilet and return to my daughter.

There's a small window on the far wall. Abby has her nose pressed to the glass. I walk over and stand there, peering over her shoulder. The azure sky before us is a dazzling sight, but I shiver at the idea of the ship drifting further away from shore, knowing I'm going to lose sight of land.

I've always tried to see the world through my daughter's eyes, and this trip is just another version of that, I suppose. I take a deep breath and focus on this moment—just this moment—before everything changes. "Can we go on deck?" Abby asks eagerly.

"Sure, but we need to swap out and charge the battery in your concentrator first."

She turns and grins at me. "It's already done."

Later, we explore the main deck, eventually making our way up to the sky lounge where passengers line the railings, watching as the ship sails further out to sea. Abby and I stand watching everything on shore get smaller and smaller. The sun sets, and from this vantage point, it is a mesmerizing sight.

Abby sighs. "This is so beautiful." She doesn't even bat an eye when the crew delivers me a second whiskey and then another. "And to think, we shouldn't even be here."

I glance over at her, but she's staring out at the water. She's right. We shouldn't be here. But I know this is not what she means. She's thinking about how lucky she is to be on this trip. I'm cursing the reason behind it all. "Please don't be sad, okay?"

"I'm not sad," I lie.

"I want this to be fun," she says. "For the both of us."

"It is fun." Another lie, but she looks relieved, so I keep it up. "I think this is the most beautiful sunset I've ever seen."

"It's probably the whiskey," she says, and we both laugh. I pull her in for a side hug and kiss the top of her head. We stand there in contentment, watching the sun melt into the horizon until there's nothing left but the stars in the night sky. They twinkle like little fireflies, as if they're looking right at us. My heart swells with love for my daughter, her beauty and innocence radiating from her like a beam of hope.

Later, when we return to our cabin, I am surprised I don't feel anxious anymore. I only have one thought: make her last wish as special as can be.

5

Abby

The ship, with its sprawling decks and glowing lights, is a thing of beauty. I can't believe I talked Dad into this trip. He's terrified of the ocean—or, any body of water where he can't see the bottom.

He says he had a bad experience as a child, but I think he's just plain ol' scared. He can't swim, but he doesn't want anyone to know. Not even me.

I step through the steamy air of the pool area and see people scattered around the deck chairs, enjoying the cool night air and the gentle sway of the ocean. I wish I had the courage to find a spot by the pool and take a dip, but I'm too shy to even think about it. Plus, Dad and the doctors agreed, it's best if my cannula stays put on this trip. They don't want my body working any harder than it should, and I am to take zero risks at least until we're back on dry land.

I want to explore the rest of the ship, but Roger says I'm not allowed to go anywhere without an adult. And by *adult,* he means *him,* because who else is there? He also says I'm not allowed to refer to him by his first name, but I don't listen to that rule, either. I begged him to let me go to the spa alone. He said no, citing safety concerns. I'm sure he's right, but I was still disappointed. I should have just let him raid the mini bar like he wanted to. *Why didn't I think of that then?*

So he walks me to the spa, and I get all checked-in and everything. Then, when I'm sure Roger has gone back to the cabin, I tell the attendant I'm not feeling well and I duck out. I'm almost shocked it worked!

I exit the spa and turn right. Back to the pool I go. Not to swim. But I have a feeling I'll find what I'm looking for there. It doesn't take me long to get back and I'm not even out of breath when I arrive. It might be day one, but I know the Grand Pacifica like the back of my hand, so I know all the best shortcuts. There's no doubt I could find my way around this ship blindfolded. I've studied the maps online for months. When you're lying around in a hospital bed, there's only so much you can do.

I find a lounge chair far enough away that I don't look weird—since I'm not dressed for swimming—but close enough that I can still see who's coming and going. Two white-haired women occupy the chairs next to mine.

"It's too noisy here, Darlene. I think I'm going to turn in."

"I'll just be a minute, then," the woman replies, which surprises me because I thought she might be asleep. "I like the fresh air."

"Suit yourself. I'll see you at breakfast."

I watch the woman walk away and wonder what it would be like to get old.

"Is she gone?"

"What?"

"I said, is she gone?"

"Um, yeah, I mean, she's heading for the elevator."

"Thank God," the woman says. Her eyes pop open. "I thought she'd never leave."

I shrug.

The woman pushes herself up onto her elbows with a pained expression. "Where are your parents, honey?"

"At dinner. I wanted some fresh air."

"Well, you should be careful. This ship may look safe, but I wouldn't let my guard down, if you know what I mean."

I don't know what she means. "I'm dying, anyway."

Her eyes widen. "Well, I assume you want to go peacefully."

"*You* don't seem too concerned."

"Me?" She swats at the air. "Oh honey, I'm old. Getting old is hell."

"The alternative isn't so great, either."

She laughs at that, tells me her name is Darlene, as though I hadn't heard the other woman say it. She asks me if this is my first cruise. "First and only," I say.

She gives me some tips and talks about the best places to visit at each port. Then Darlene lies back in her lounge chair and insists that I tell her about myself. She says she has trouble falling asleep ever since Ernie died.

The thing is, I don't have many stories, and the ones I do have consist mostly of hospitals and tests and a lot of waiting. So, I tell her how I've always wanted to take a cruise. I tell her about how Mom used to have these travel brochures she kept around the house. I never really gave it much thought, but I guess she was looking for a good reason to leave, even then.

Darlene nods as if what I've just said is the most natural thing in the world. Then she looks straight at me and lowers her voice. "So, you've heard about what happened on this ship a few months ago, then?"

6

Abby

"Now, who is this you're talking about?" Darlene asks. Her eyelids flutter open and then close again.

"My mother," I say. "But what did you mean about what happened on this ship a few months ago?"

She completely ignores my question, but maybe she's hard of hearing. Or maybe she's like my Grammy was before she passed, and her memory has given out. "It didn't sound like your mother..."

"She wasn't like most mothers," I say. "At night, she didn't read me fables or fairy tales. She read me travel brochures."

"How strange," Darlene remarks. But it wasn't strange. The diner where she worked kept them in one of those file stands at the entrance. I used to help put them back in place whenever I had to tag along with Mom to work, which was a lot.

"In my day, a woman's place was in the home. But everything's different now..."

I understand what Darlene is saying. I can't blame Mama for wanting better for herself than Lucky's Diner. She always said she wanted to travel the world. And I guess she finally found her way.

I wanted to find mine. Who would have guessed it would have been on a charity trip, because I'm a kid with a terminal illness?

"You never know how life's going to pan out," I tell Darlene, because that's what Mama used to say.

"No, you don't."

"I guess I was interested in seeing what the big deal was. I remember all those glossy photos with happy, smiling families. Although, that's only half of it. I may be sick, but I still have a few goals of my own. I just sort of hoped I'd have more time to see them through, you know?"

Darlene murmurs something incoherently, and I wonder if she's fallen asleep.

"Maybe my mother is the smart one," I say. "Maybe Roger's right, even if I'd never admit it. Maybe I *am* borrowing her dream. I want to see the world, but more than that, I want to know this isn't it for me. I don't want to die in some no-name town with two traffic lights, always known as 'that sick girl.' At least for this week, on *this* ship, I want to believe that *anything* is possible. That I can have whatever I want with a snap of my fingers."

Darlene nods, eyes still closed. "That sounds lovely, dear."

"More than anything, I want to see my mother one last time."

I tell Darlene how Roger thinks Mom's living on some pot farm up in Oregon, because that's what she wants him to think. But she's not. She's somewhere on this ship. Working, or at least she was two months ago.

And even if she's not onboard, I have other motives to fill my time. I learned from Mama's emails that there's no better place for a brief romance than on cruise ships, and I desperately want to fall in love.

Instantly, I feel silly for admitting that out loud, and I wish I could take it back. I'm hoping Darlene is forgetful like my

Grammy, that or she really is hard of hearing and it's not all an act.

"Darlene?" I glance over, noticing the way her chest barely rises and falls. *Is she even breathing?* I lean forward and shake her, hard.

Her eyes pop open and she springs up like a Jack-in-the-box. "What? What is it?"

"Thank God," I breathe, heart still pounding. "I thought you were—"

When she recovers from her momentary panic, she says, "It's that virus they keep talking about. It's scaring the living daylights out of everyone."

"Virus?"

"I told Ethel, it's halfway around the world, for God's sake. And we're on a ship. You know how it is. They always make a big deal over nothing. Anyway—" she leans back in her chair, eyes already closing. "That's a nice story you were telling, dear. Keep going."

Once I'm certain she's asleep, I say that I have to find my parents, even though I know she doesn't hear me.

I check the time, realizing I need to get back to the spa, just in case Roger shows up early. I walk from one end of the deck to the other and grab a chair because I feel short of breath.

As I stand there huffing, I notice a group of teenage boys nearby. One of them catches my eye and smiles at me. My cheeks flush in response. *Maybe God really is listening.* Not knowing what else to do, because saying hi would involve talking to someone my age for the first time in months—something that terrifies me! I sit there, trying to pretend like I haven't even noticed him.

Suddenly, a voice calls out. "Hey! Want to join us?" A small group of people are gathered around a table and are playing cards or board games or something. They look friendly enough, so I decide to take a chance.

As I approach, I notice a strange symbol printed on their

shirts. The symbol is shaped like a jagged star, with five points and a circle in the center. I ask what it means and am told I'll "find out in time."

"I haven't got much time," I say.

The green-eyed boy flashes me a mischievous smirk. "None of us do."

I hesitate, knowing I need to get back before Roger finds out what I've done. I plan to spend a lot of time at the "spa" this week, and I don't want to mess things up on the first day.

But then the boy with emerald eyes looks straight at me, and I know I'm not going to walk away. At least not yet.

"Okay," I hear myself whisper. "I'm in."

Just then, I feel a hand on my shoulder. I turn and see a man wearing a similar shirt. He's tall and muscular, and he looks at me with a stern expression.

"You don't want to get involved here," he says.

I open my mouth to respond, but nothing comes out. I'm too stunned to speak. What is he talking about? I shake my head, and he quickly takes his hand away.

"It's not safe," he says, almost in a whisper. "Trust me."

Then he turns around and walks away, leaving me standing there, trying to figure out what just happened.

7

Roger

Making my way through the noisy throng of people, I search for a place to wait while Abby enjoys her spa visit. I'm used to waiting around for her appointments, but this feels different. This should be a joyous time, and the thought of Abby not having her mother by her side causes me to sink into a deep dark hole of despair.

But I know better than to follow that train of thought down the rabbit hole. It never leads to anything good. In the end, the result is the same. Abby is still without a mother, and Morgan is still MIA. Though I guess that's not technically correct. I know where Morgan is, even if she'd rather not be found.

The last thing I want is to be alone in a cabin with thoughts like these, so I decide to explore the ship. After a few wrong turns, I eventually stumble upon a bar and I make a beeline for it. After ordering a drink, I sit down and stare out toward the abyss of the dark sea.

From the corner of my eye, I notice a man staring in my direction. He's looking for conversation, which I am not in the mood for.

"Do you come here often?" he asks. His voice is deep and commanding.

I turn to him, not sure how to respond. But then I see he is joking. I'd laugh for the sake of politeness, but I'm not looking for company.

"No," I reply curtly.

He grins at me and inclines his head, as if he can sense my aversion to talking. "Beautiful night," he says, gesturing to the window.

I take a sip of my drink and nod. The whiskey warms me from the inside and I try my best to forget all my troubles on land. "Yeah."

He laughs like he gets me. "I'm Blake," he says, holding out his hand.

"Roger."

He lifts his beer bottle and signals the bartender for another. "You don't seem like the cruiser type, Roger."

"No." I sigh. "This was my daughter's idea. I'm just along for the ride."

"What do you do? For a living, if you don't mind me asking."

"I'm a mechanic."

He grins. "Oh, yeah?"

I shrug. "You?"

"Tech. Nothing special."

I don't press him for details, since I'm not interested.

The bartender pushes a new bottle toward him, and he tilts it, studying the label. "Roger, how's a mechanic afford a trip like this?"

A man two stools down leans sideways, drunkenly waving his hand in the air as if he's been waiting for this moment all his life. "When's the last time you've had your car worked on?"

"Fair point."

I turn to Blake and say, "I'm here for my daughter. To give her a chance to make memories that will last a lifetime. My lifetime. She likely won't make it to eighteen. This trip—it's one of those wish fulfillment things."

"Jesus." He takes a swig of his beer and shakes his head. "That sucks."

I shrug. "It is what it is."

Without warning, the man next to Blake crumples to the ground. I'm stunned by the suddenness of it. Blake leaps off his stool to come to the man's aid, assuming he just fainted. But when he looks up at me with wide eyes and a gaping mouth, I realize this isn't the case. "I think he's dead," Blake whispers.

My pulse quickens, and I feel a dizzying sensation run down my limbs. I scramble off my barstool and crouch down to check for a pulse. My stomach sinks. "Shit."

"Dead, right?" Blake says.

I start CPR.

"I thought you said you were a mechanic," he says as I kneel over the man pumping his chest.

Breathlessly, I say, "I also said my daughter's sick."

"You're wasting your time." Blake repeats himself as if maybe I hadn't heard the first time. "I'm pretty sure he's dead."

I ignore him and keep going. "If I stop, he will be for sure."

8

Roger

I scan the lounge and the next thing I know, I'm shouting. "Anyone call for help?"

The bartender leans over the counter. "Medical's on the way."

Blake runs his fingers through his hair. “They have designated freezers for the dead ones, you know.”

I keep pumping away, Blake keeps talking. "The old ones," he says. "They come on these cruises and just keel over. You wouldn’t believe how common it is. These ships, most of them, have morgues."

People cluster around, trying to figure out what happened.

"It's not an accident, that's for sure," a woman claims. "This must be, what…the fifth one?”

The lady next to her agrees. “Something's going on.”

"I heard the ship is half empty on account of that virus going around over in Asia. They say it might spread stateside too."

"You're so paranoid, Martha," her companion scoffs. "I swear, it's something different with you every other week."

"Well, I was not going to let it keep me away," she says. "But it seems like a lot of people are more paranoid than me."

"You're relieved, mister," the bartender says, and I realize he's talking to me. I've been pumping and listening to those women for too long. Sweat's pouring down my back, and the crowd's thicker than I thought. The bartender's standing right behind me now. "I've got it from here."

"I have to go," I say, pushing myself up. I take off in the spa's direction. I don't know what it is, but I have the sense I need to see my daughter. Now.

When I reach the spa, the attendant looks perplexed. She says Abby left shortly after checking in, said she wasn't feeling well. "Would you like me to ring your cabin?"

Dread settles in my stomach. "Yes, please."

I wonder if Abby will even think about picking up if she is there. Kids these days. All they know is texting. But also, if she's feeling bad, she may not be able to answer. She may not have even been able to make it back. How stupid of me to leave her here. What was I thinking?

I tap the desk. "Is there a way to see if her swipe card was used to enter the room?"

"Um... not here, I'm afraid. But I can call security if you'd like."

"She's not answering?"

The woman shakes her head.

"Yeah, call security and medical. I'll meet them there."

I sprint through the decks, through the hallways, checking every corner. Panic seeps through my veins, I'm desperate to find her and make sure she's okay. My mind races through every scenario. Maybe the battery on her oxygen concentrator was low. Usually, we can get three hours out of a charge, but sometimes it's not consistent. Maybe she's seasick. Or maybe she's coming down with something. It would be just our luck…

When I reach deck four, I pause in my tracks.

Abby is talking to a man—or rather, the man is saying something to her. She looks stricken, and then she glances around at a group of teenagers.

She doesn't look sick; she looks uncertain. Relief washes over me like a wave, though I'm now filled with an overwhelming sense of worry about the questionable company she's keeping. I approach her, and she turns toward me with a wary expression.

"Abby," I say, trying to keep my voice from shaking. "What are you doing here?"

She has a deer in the headlights look. "Dad."

I check her over. "You're not sick."

I can tell by the expression on my daughter's face that we both know she has been caught in a lie. "You can breathe? Your battery's not dead?"

I check the gauge. It shows a 75 percent charge.

She casts her gaze down, avoiding my eyes. When she speaks, her voice is barely audible. "I just wanted to see what it was like."

"Come on," I say, taking her by the arm. "Let's go."

As we make our way back to our cabin, I can't help but feel a sense of unease. I'm not sure what might have happened if I hadn't come upon her when I did, but I know I have to keep her safe. Little did I know, the danger was just beginning.

9

Passenger 327

The situation is growing more and more bizarre by the minute. The problem, as I see it, is that we have it too easy nowadays. It took little time to uncover the dark past of the beautifully enticing woman I encountered yesterday. Jenna Hill. With a few strokes of a keyboard, I know almost everything about her. And just like that, it all makes sense.

Fascinating story, really. Jenna had a boyfriend named Bo, who had a sister named Heather. Unfortunately, that is no longer the case since Jenna decided to drink and drive, claiming the lives of both Heather and Bo. The parents of this dead pair are as bitter as they come. They will give anything to see justice served for their children's murderer. To add insult to injury, Jenna is being mischaracterized as some sort of fiend, and she is certainly not supposed to be on this ship—which is why my plan for her is even more satisfying.

But I'm not ready to end her life yet. Not when I can savor her misery. Besides, I'm already eyeing another target. Heard him at the bar last night chattering about a sick child, car repairs, and all that. Some dude just keels over in that bar, and this guy, he just stands there chatting away like nothing happened.

That got me thinking, why would someone just stand there and do nothing? He wouldn't. Not unless he was trying to lay low. Want to know why I think so?

Well, his name is Blake. Blake Nelson. It wasn't easy digging up info on him. Believe me, I was up half the night trying to do it. Don't know his story yet. But I will soon enough.

Unless I kill him before that. I get bored so easily.

But back to the bizarre part. Last night, while I was trying to get the scoop on Nelson, I needed a break and went out to get some fresh air and maybe a cup of coffee.

I felt a strange, uncomfortable feeling, as I stared at my next victim.

It was a woman, her back facing me, making her way down to the lower decks. I had seen her around the corridors, always alone, but never had I seen her like this...

And suddenly, I couldn't stop watching her. It's not just curiosity—there's something about her that draws me in.

The next thing I know, I'm following her into the depths of the ship, hungering for knowledge about this mysterious woman.

The woman, Molly, she never looks back as she slowly makes her way toward the ship's smaller theater. It's empty at this early hour of the morning. Or at least it should be.

It seems to be a secret room known only to the cultists on board. I had seen them around the ship, but not this many all in one place.

They gather around a large circle of candles, murmuring a strange incantation. I watch in awe as the woman steps into the circle and bows her head before them.

I can see their leader, a tall figure with a hood obscuring his face, save for a pair of piercing eyes.

“Let us welcome our new sister, Molly.” His voice is calm and yet somehow it manages to chill my bones. Molly bows her head again, as if in reverence.

A reflexive gasp escapes me as I watch the cultists perform some sort of ritual sacrifice. I want to look away, but I cannot.

Molly seems to be chosen to be the sacrificial offering and I want to speak in protest, as she is meant to be mine, but I know it will do no good.

I watch helplessly from backstage, mesmerized by the unfolding events.

The leader speaks in an eerie voice, “We gather here so that I, Isaac the Enlightened, may marry Molly Bloom. And by doing so, we must offer another woman to the gods.”

He snaps his fingers, and a figure is produced.

"Please bring her forward," he commands in a tone that leaves no room for refusal.

The woman stands strapped to the altar, wearing a white dress that brings out her pale complexion. Her mouth is taped shut, and tears stream down her face. I can't make out what the leader intones, but the sound of the chanting swells in intensity.

The cultists then carry her from the theater and out to the open-air deck. She doesn't fight them or drag her feet; she's resigned to her fate.

A chill passes through me when I see one of them take out a pocketknife and carve a symbol into the woman's forehead. An incantation is uttered, and then they lift her up and toss her overboard.

The acrid smell of blood hangs in the air when they leave, and I stand there in shock at what I've seen—a human sacrifice right before my eyes.

10

Abby

Everything shifts in an instant. Dad has been on his laptop for hours, the red veins in his eyes becoming more pronounced as the minutes tick by. His movements are tense with agitation, and he paces from one end of the cabin to the other like a caged animal. We were supposed to dock in Nassau later today, but it is looking increasingly unlikely as news of the coronavirus spreads across the world. Dad's glued to the news, switching back and forth between various sites incessantly. Every few minutes it seems there's some new revelation. Countries are closing their borders, flights are being canceled, and there are reports of hospitals soon being overwhelmed.

Dad looks up at me. His face is pale and sweaty, his dark hair sticking up in tufts, his eyes wide and wild. "This is very bad, Abby."

"I'm sure it will be fine."

He shakes his head and exhales before returning to frantically tapping away at the keyboard of his laptop, pausing only to stare out the cabin window with a faraway look. Finally, he gets up and crosses the room.

"The captain is going to make an announcement shortly. Not that it really matters what he says—the writing's on the wall."

Dad speaks as if life as we know it is over.

"It's not forever," I say in a bid to reassure him. "Just fifteen days to slow the spread."

Roger slumps down on the bed. "How did I not see this coming?"

I think back to my encounter with the old lady, Darlene, the night before. "This must be what she was talking about last night...."

Roger's head pops up out of his hands, and he looks at me with a weary expression. "Who?"

I ignore him. I'm thinking about the boy with the green eyes, and that man's warning. Now it makes sense. I feel stupid for being so creeped out.

"Abigail—what are you talking about?"

"Nothing. Just some old lady I met last night. She was talking about the virus and bad stuff happening on the ship. I thought she was just crazy."

He looks angry, and I'm not sure why. "You know what this means, don't you?"

I look at him expectantly. "What?"

"It means we've possibly been exposed."

I sit in stunned silence. I knew Roger was concerned about this trip on account of my disease, but it hadn't occurred to me that this could happen. The thought of being ill on a ship in the middle of the ocean is enough to make my stomach churn. It does not sound like a fun way to die.

"We need to get off this boat," Dad says, his voice tight with worry. "We need to be near a hospital."

"Could you please calm down?"

"Don't tell me to calm down! Do you have any idea—" He stands up and starts pacing again. "We have to stay away from people, and the only way to do that is to stay in this cabin."

I can't believe what I'm hearing. "But what about the Bahamas? Grand Turk?"

"Abby, I don't think you understand."

"I'm not staying in this cabin for that long!" I say. "Being cooped up in here sounds like a nightmare! It sounds like prison."

"You really don't get it."

"Oh, I get it. You're overreacting like you always do!"

"Someone died last night—in the bar. I gave him CPR. That means I've been exposed."

"You were in the bar? I knew it!"

"Abigail—"

"You promised."

"Yeah, well, you promised you'd be at the spa and look how that turned out."

"I told you—I *was* at the spa!"

"Stop." Roger walks over to the window. "None of this matters. They're not going to let us dock. Not until the virus is contained," he says miserably. He's getting agitated again, running his hands through his hair. "We may have to stay at sea for weeks, maybe months."

My stomach drops. This is not the vacation I was expecting. "I think you're overthinking it. They can't keep us here."

"Technically, they can."

"How can you know that?"

"I just have a gut feeling," he says.

"Your gut is overreacting," I tell him, but I'm wrong.

The captain's announcement comes a few minutes later. We're not going to Nassau. We're heading back to Miami. We'll be quarantined onboard for the next fourteen days, and no one is allowed off the boat.

11

Passenger 327

I hear the voices of passengers before I even see them. Arguing and debating, pleading and negotiating. The conversations wash over me, each one more desperate than the last. I almost can't believe my luck.

I am confident my cabin is situated in the most interesting of corridors. These people. You would not believe it.

First, I overhear the bickering between the guy and his sick kid. The man, Roger, is determined to get off the ship, while his daughter believes they should stay.

"We can't just sit here and do nothing!" he says. "We should be looking for a way out of here!"

"And what if we can't find a way off the ship? We have to consider the risks."

"I know the risks," Roger snaps. "But if we stay here, we could be facing something much worse than the virus."

His daughter scoffs. "I don't even know what that means."

"And I pray you don't find out."

The argument continues on like this, neither side willing to budge. I can't help but feel a sense of excitement as I listen. The only thing better than committing murder is watching other people do it. There's something about the way their voices quiver and shake that makes me wonder which is going to be the first to go. My money is on the father. He oughta grow a pair and put that girl in her place. But what do I know? I hate kids.

As I wander the ship, I overhear more conversations. Some are between families and friends, discussing what to do in this uncertain time. Others are between complete strangers, desperate to find a way out of their current predicament. I hear so many rumors, so much hearsay, that by the end of it, I don't know what to think.

I'm too distracted to care. My mind keeps drifting back to what I saw on deck last night. I pay extra attention to anyone wearing one of those ridiculous shirts with the symbols.

Eventually, I stumble upon a group of teenagers, and it isn't long before I find out what's really going on. Their leader, "Isaac the Enlightened," has called a special meeting. When the boys speak, their words are confident and sure, as if they have already resigned themselves to the shadows of the future. As for the meeting, I have nothing better to do, so I figure I might as well eavesdrop on that, too.

I can't help but roll my eyes as I listen to this guy spout his nonsense. He talks about how the virus is a sign of the end times, and how the only way to survive is to embrace the darkness. His followers nod along, eagerly soaking up his words like sponges. Many of them are just kids, too young to know any better. But I know better. I've seen true darkness, and it's not something you want to embrace.

Later, I notice a girl in the group staring at me. She's pretty, with long blonde hair and bright blue eyes. I can tell she is interested in me, but I'm not interested in her. She's too young for my taste. But that doesn't stop me from playing along.

I give her a sly grin. "What are you staring at?"

"Nothing," she says, blushing. "I was just wondering if you wanted to join our group."

"Oh, really?" I feign interest. "What's your group all about?"

"We're preparing for the end times." Her voice is filled with conviction. "We believe that the darkness is coming, and the only way to survive is to embrace it."

I can't help but laugh. She parrots her leader well. "That's cute," I say. "But I've seen darkness, and it's not something you want to embrace."

Her eyes widen with curiosity. "What do you mean?"

"I mean that the darkness is real." I drop my voice to a whisper. "And it's coming for all of us."

The girl leans in closer, her breath hot on my neck. I can feel her body heat as she presses against me.

"Tell me more," she whispers.

I glance around the deck, making sure no one is watching us. Then I lean in close to her ear. "I've seen things you can't even imagine. Things that would make your skin crawl."

She shivers, but doesn't pull away.

"I've seen people do unspeakable things," I continue. "Things that would make you sick to your stomach."

"What kind of things?"

"Things like torture," I say. "And murder. And worse."

She gasps, but still doesn't pull away. I have a feeling she's seen these things, too. Or that she will soon. I'm a little surprised at her approach. What a cunning little liar.

"And the darkness?" she asks. "What about the darkness?"

I pause for a moment, considering how much to reveal, considering it's clear she's a snake.

"The darkness is seductive," I say finally. "It promises power beyond your wildest dreams. But it comes at a cost."

"What cost?"

"The cost of your soul. Once you accept it, there's no going back."

She looks at me with wide eyes, her expression a mixture of fear and fascination.

"Do you want to know more?" I ask, my voice low and dangerous.

Her voice is barely audible when she speaks. "Yes."

"Then meet me tonight," I say. "On the observation deck. And maybe I'll consider joining your group."

12

Roger

The third day on the ship feels different. Electric energy hangs in the air, with a sense of danger and uncertainty.

I awake from my fitful sleep, and as I peer out my cabin window, all I can see are choppy waves and rolling black clouds—a stark contrast to the tranquil waters from yesterday.

The cabin is silent. Then voices drift in from outside my cabin—panicked passengers competing for attention with desperate cries and accusations.

I throw on a shirt and open my door to investigate. A dozen people are gathered around a crew member in the central hallway. They plead and shout, their air of desperation palpable.

The crew member holds his hands up, trying to calm them. "Please," he says in a low, steady voice. "I understand your concerns, but I ask you to remain calm. We are doing everything we can to ensure your safety and comfort."

I attempt to make my way through the oppressive crowd, but a towering figure blocks my path. The throng of passengers is thick, and I have to avoid them because of Abby's fragile state.

"I don't understand," the man bellows. "What plans have you made to keep us safe? How can we stay afloat when there's no port to dock in? And what about provisions?"

The crew member doesn't answer. His eyes widen in fear as his mouth hangs agape.

"I have dietary restrictions!" a woman shouts.

"I need my mineral water," another woman hisses. "You tell the captain he's going to have to make this right!"

The crowd becomes restless; their voices rise like a chorus of angry hyenas, shouting questions such as, "Where is the food? How much water do we have? What aren't you telling us?"

He avoids their prying eyes, nervously clearing his throat before attempting to speak, but another voice from the back of the mob interrupts him. "We want answers! Tell us the truth or else! We can't just stay here and hope for the best."

The staff member cowers in terror as the passengers move forward, forming a menacing circle around him. I feel the tension in the air as they wait for his response that never comes.

Suddenly, one passenger steps forward, seizing him by the shoulders. He shakes the man violently while shouting in his face: "Tell us now or we will beat it out of you! We demand to know what is really going on! How much food do you have left? How much water? Do you have my wife's mineral water or no? What supplies? Speak now or suffer!"

The trembling crew member barely stammers out a response: "We have enough food and water for several weeks… We are doing all we can…please be patient..."

But it's too late. No one believes him; the crowd has descended into a frenzied rage, with wild fists and screams filling the air. I consider ducking back inside my room and locking the door. But I need answers all the same.

Another angry man straightens his shoulders and steps

forward. "We have to make a choice," he says, his voice ringing out over the chaos. "We can either sit here and hope for help to arrive, or we can fight for our survival."

The crowd jeers, but he remains resolute. "I say we fight," he says firmly. "We can't just give up."

"We must kill him," the woman says, and I think her "dietary restrictions" have driven her mad. "We must set an example! Charles is right, we must fight!"

I want to ask what they're fighting for but I am apparently alone in my thoughts. Her words strike a chord with the other passengers as they erupt in agreement, their voices growing louder and more aggressive.

"All right," he says. "We'll start making preparations for whatever is necessary to ensure our survival." The crowd is somewhat mollified by the call to action.

"We need a leader," he says. "Someone to take charge."

"I'll do it," a woman answers out of the blue. "Just let him go and I'll get you the answers you need."

The man eyes her suspiciously. "How can we trust you?"

She stares into his eyes with an icy glare as she replies, "What choice do you have? I guess you could finish what you started and spend the rest of your life in prison. But just so you know, this ship you're on, it's registered out of Barbados. So don't expect some fancy American prison."

The man's jaw clenches as he loosens his grip on the crew member, unnerved by her words.

"Do what I say," he spits at the man through gritted teeth, "or else."

"I'd leave it there if I were you," the woman says, a sly smirk playing across her lips that sends a chill through us all.

He complies, and the crew member scurries away. I duck back into the cabin and take a deep breath. This situation is a prime example of the irrationality of collective behavior—where key issues are decided for superficial reasons.

Based on the news reports, I don't see it getting better anytime soon. A tempest of emotions sweeps through me. I think about how similar situations must be playing out all over the ship—people making irrational decisions without consequence. I know from my stint in the Army that it will only get worse.

This is a powder keg of a situation, and my decision has to be made now. One glance at my sleeping daughter and I know the answer. I am determined to fight for our survival—whatever the cost might be.

13

Abby

I jerk awake to the sound of the waves crashing against the side of the ship. The low hum of the TV flickers from the corner. Roger's doing, I'm sure, but he's nowhere to be seen.

A surge of energy rushes through me, sudden and invigorating, like I haven't felt for years.

I leap out of bed and race to the window, throwing open the curtains. A vast ocean stands before me, stretching endlessly in every direction, with no sign of land on the horizon.

My heart leaps as my dad's words echo through my mind: *I'm meeting with the captain in the morning. We need to discuss a plan to get you off this ship because of your weakened immune system.*

I laughed at the conviction in his voice. As if half the passengers onboard aren't also in the same predicament. Most of them are ancient.

I scramble into some clothes, eager to seize my chance before

Roger returns and ruins it all. I know I'm being hard on him, but being trapped in this cabin together is making us both crazy. Virus or no virus, I have to get out of here before I lose my mind.

As I slip out into the hallway, everything seems different—quieter, darker. I take the elevator to deck five and slip into the staff corridor as a crew member hurries out. I'm half expecting someone who passes to tell me I shouldn't be here, but no one does. People hardly notice me at all. Everyone seems to be in some sort of stupor, as if someone has turned smoke on a beehive.

Out of the corner of my eye, I spot a man loitering in a doorway, his eyes trained on me with an intensity that makes me want to turn back. *This is it.* I'm about to get busted.

I already have my speech all worked out. It's so easy to get lost on this ship. I almost chicken out and turn back, but I keep moving. Something inside propels me onward—who knows when I'll get another opportunity?

I move forward, and the man steps out of the shadows.

He's tall and lanky, wearing jeans, a T-shirt, and a wide-brimmed hat. His eyes are almost too large for his face, as he scrutinizes me with suspicion.

"You're looking for something," he rasps in a low voice.

I barely manage to force the words past my dry throat. "Yes. I'm looking for my mother."

The man nods slowly. "I see," he says. "Well, I may be able to help you."

My heart races, and I feel my skin prickle as I realize who he is — he's from that strange group with the obscure symbols on their shirts. Usually, he's flanked by a handful of gorgeous women, so it's surprising to see him alone.

"I'm Isaac," he says with a curt nod.

"Abby."

Isaac smiles devilishly. I take it he's not supposed to be here either. "Ahh, yes. Abby. Now I remember. I heard my friend Jacob was quite taken with you. From the other night at the pool?"

The boy with the green eyes flashes in my mind. I shrug. "I've met a lot of people. It's a big ship."

"I'm sure you have questions," he says. "Perhaps I can help you find some answers."

I shake my head hastily and step away from him. "No, I'd better get back—my dad's waiting for me."

He smirks knowingly. "Your dad is on the bridge."

"The what?"

"He's speaking with the captain."

"Oh, right. He had a meeting," I say, trying to make Roger sound important, though I don't know why. I'm mortified at how much I'm spilling to this stranger, yet despite it all, I can't seem to shut up. It's like every detail of my life has come pouring out through my mouth without permission. With trembling lips, I quickly tell him about my cystic fibrosis and why I can't be around people—my compromised immune system—why Roger is trying desperately to get us off the boat before it's too late.

His smile turns devious, and he hisses, "Sweetheart, none of us are getting off this ship. But tell you what—I'll tell Jacob you said hello."

My heart slams in my chest at his words. *Jacob*. The boy with the green eyes. What does he have to do with this? And why does this Isaac guy think he knows everything?

Isaac takes a step toward me, invading my personal space. His face is inches away from mine, and I can smell his musky cologne.

"You know, you're a very pretty girl," he says, his eyes burning into mine. "I'm sure you could have any of my friends you wanted."

I step back, my heart racing. "I don't want your friends," I say firmly. "I just want to find my mother."

Isaac chuckles. "Like I said, I'm sure I can help you with that, too."

"No thanks."

"Suit yourself," he shrugs. His gesture makes me realize how much I sounded like a child just now. "But if you change your mind, you know where to find me."

He melts into the shadows, leaving me alone in the hallway. Questions cloud my thoughts, but I don't have time for contemplation. I need to focus on finding Mom before Roger comes back. If he finds out I've been within six feet of anyone, he'll lose his mind. For real. He keeps going on and on about everyone being infected. Something about them being *asymptomatic.* I'm worried about his mental state, and even though I don't want to cut our vacation short, I'm sort of hoping the captain gives him good news. I don't know how much longer either one of us can handle his paranoia.

I continue down the hallway, my heart pounding with each step. As I turn a corner, I see a door at the end of the hallway. It's slightly ajar. I can hear a radio playing inside.

I approach the door, pushing it open with a trembling hand. I'm not supposed to be here, but if anyone will know how to find Morgan Atkins, it'll be one of the crew members. I've asked a few already, but no one has given me anything definite. Darlene said the cruise line hires thousands of people and apparently, the crews on these ships are never the same.

But I know my mother was here as of two months ago. And even if it seems stupid and naive, this is the closest I've come to her in years. To know she walked these same halls, it may sound silly, but it makes me feel close to her.

"Hello?"

The room is illuminated by a single lamp. A bunk bed is against the far wall, and a woman lying on the lower bunk catches my eye. She's sprawled out on her back, eyes wide open and fixed on nothing. I assumed she was sleeping, but reason tells me otherwise. Her skin has turned waxy and pale. She's been dead for some time now.

My breath catches in my throat as fear takes hold. Did Isaac just emerge from this room? Or was it the next one? Is Roger right? Is the virus spreading across the ship?

I want to flee, but shock pins me in place, and I'm unable to move or speak. Tears blur my vision and despair grips me as I realize that this could very well be me. Or Dad. I know I have to get back. If this virus doesn't kill me, Roger will. Which is how I know I can never, ever tell him what I've just seen.

14

Passenger 327

I grip the railing, sweat beading on my brow. I've been here for an hour, waiting and watching, but there's still no sign of her. I tell myself it's fate. It's because she's too young. Even *I* have some scruples. Sure, I was probably going to kill her, but really, I just wanted to find out more about this cult. I don't handle competition very well.

Fifteen minutes pass. A deep-seated anger builds inside me—people these days are so unreliable. Overhead, laughter tinkles like a bell, but it's not her laughter. As I wait, uneasiness twists in my stomach. Someone is playing games with me.

My gaze flicks to a bottle of vodka tucked between two lifeboats. It's those teenagers' doing, no doubt. I step forward, overwhelmed by a strange urge to take a swig. The taste lingers longer than expected, as if trying to warn me. I'm growing restless; bad things will happen if I don't get a grip soon.

An odd sense of disconnection has settled over the ship—new

sanitation practices have been implemented that go largely unnoticed by most passengers, while rumors are circulating about our itinerary being changed yet again due to backlogged ships in port. We can no longer dock in Miami; instead we're stuck on this boat with no escape in sight and tension rising like flood waters.

It would still be a few hours before I'd find out what happened to the girl I was supposed to meet, but for now, my focus shifts back to sweet Jenna.

I spot her in the bar on the upper deck, just as I'd expected. The dim lighting casts a golden halo through her long, dark locks — highlighting eyes that blaze with an intensity I recognize.

My strides quicken as I make my way over to her, my heart pounding in anticipation.

"Is this taken?" I ask, gesturing at the seat next to her, though most of them are unoccupied.

She glances up from her wine glass and away without answering. Taking it as a no, I slide onto the stool and turn to face her.

"Have you heard the rumors?" I query, signaling the bartender.

Her expression remains unchanged, but I see a faint shake of her head.

"They're saying we're turning back toward Nassau."

"Great," she mutters dryly.

I offer a friendly smile. "I'm Bo."

I notice the slight twitch of her features. It's like I've sucker-punched her, but she's trying to put up a brave front. I've been waiting for this moment for days. That name not only has a ring to it, it's like a switchblade digging into her gut. "And you are?"

"Emily," she lies. My curiosity is piqued.

"Emily," I repeat slowly with a smirk on my face. "It's a pleasure to meet you."

I flash my cruise card so the bartender can scan it. "You're an artist?"

She suddenly turns and looks me up and down suspiciously. "How'd you know?"

Chuckling, I point at her hands. "There's paint under your nails—but also because I spotted you up on deck yesterday."

She raises an eyebrow, impressed. "You're observant."

"I try to be," I say with a smile. "So what brings you on this cruise?"

"Just needed to get away for a while," she says, her eyes downcast.

"I know the feeling," I say sympathetically. "But with all that's been happening on this ship, it's hard to relax, isn't it?"

Her eyes flick up to mine, and I can see the fear there. "What do you mean?"

"Well, there's all the stuff going on with the virus, and now the rumors about our itinerary being changed. It's making people restless," I say, taking a sip of my drink. "And, in my experience, when people get restless, bad things can happen."

She nods, her eyes darting around the bar nervously. "I've heard whispers about something happening to one of the passengers," she says in a hushed voice. "A young girl was just found. But there have been others."

"Yes, I heard that too," I say, leaning in closer. "But I'm more interested in what's happening between us right now."

She looks at me, her eyes darkening with desire. "What do you mean?"

"I mean that I've been watching you for days, Emily. And now that we're both here, alone, I think we should get to know each other a little better."

I place a hand on her thigh, and she doesn't pull away. The heat radiating off her skin is electric. "I'm not sure that's a good idea," she says hesitantly.

"Why not?" I ask, moving even closer. "We're trapped on this ship together, Emily. We might as well make the best of it."

She bites her lip and looks away, thinking it over. "I don't know," she says slowly. "I'm not really in a good place right now."

"I understand," I say soothingly. "But sometimes, the best way to forget your problems is to lose yourself in something else. And I promise you, Emily, I can make you forget everything except how good I can make you feel."

Her eyes flick back to mine, and I can see the hunger there. It takes several more drinks and a little pharmaceutical magic, but eventually she turns to me and says, “Okay. Let's go back to your room.”

I stand up, taking her hand in mine. "I think you'll find it's much more comfortable than this bar," I say with a grin.

As we stumble out of the bar and toward my cabin, I feel a shiver run down my spine as I think of Jenna Hill and what I'm about to do — how her life is about to change. She may be troubled, but it doesn't matter. What matters is that I'll get what I want in the end.

15

Roger

I've exhausted all my contacts on the cruise ship, with no luck. The captain and cruise director had nothing new to tell me; they just promised that if anything changed, I'd be the first to know.

A thick cloud of dread hangs over Abby and me. We try to ignore it by playing cards, watching TV, and doing her breathing treatments—but deep down we both know the truth: I can't keep her cooped up in here forever. It's too dark and stuffy, without sunlight or fresh air; if we stay inside much longer, we'll both lose our minds.

The crew members don't look too good either—their once-smiling faces are now strained with worry as rumors about running out of food and supplies start to circulate throughout the passengers. Incessant bickering breaks out between passengers over food and resources, pushing everybody's nerves to their limits. After being turned away from three ports already, we're all beginning to fear an unending journey ahead.

The cruise director promises me that someone will deliver any medication we run out of once we reach port, but nobody knows when or *where* that will be.

Adding more horror to what seems like an endless voyage, passengers are dropping dead left and right—some say it's the virus, others believe something more sinister is going on. Blake, the guy from the bar, told me there were several suspicious deaths a few months ago that nobody talks about anymore. He says the corporate office is quick to squash anything that might put the cruise line in jeopardy, and that things get buried fairly efficiently. He sounds like a journalist to me, but no, he's in tech.

And if that weren't enough, rumors concerning a cult onboard seep through the cracks of every conversation. I've noticed them —they usually stay together and most of them wear black T-shirts adorned with an orange symbol—but until now I hadn't paid much attention. Now they've become a source of suspicion, too.

Blake tells me stories of people locked away in cabins and strange symbols painted on walls in the night. There are tales of invite-only gatherings with members wearing white robes and hoods, chanting in a foreign tongue or muttering incantations as they stalk through the hallways like ghosts.

Determined to find out what is going on, I decide to take matters into my own hands and confront the captain again. But when I arrive at the bridge, I can tell something is off—the door hangs ajar and chaos reigns inside. Papers litter the ground, and the captain's hat lays forgotten on the floor. He lies in the middle of it all, lifeless, as crew members hover around him, speaking in hushed voices about some kind of medical emergency.

The ship grows so still that it almost feels like it's holding its breath. Fear and tension fill the air, suffocating me like a cloud waiting for a storm. Desperate for answers, I approach the group and ask in a hushed whisper, "What's going on?"

One of them turns to me and shakes his head. "We don't know yet. The captain collapsed, and we can't seem to revive him. We've called for a doctor, but no one knows when they'll be able to arrive."

My heart sinks further as I realize that our already precarious situation has just become even more dire. Without a captain, who will guide the ship? Who will be in charge of securing supplies and maintaining order among the passengers?

I whirl around to Abby, who is standing beside me, her face as pale as milk. "We've gotta get off this ship," I tell her.

But Abby shakes her head. "Where would we go?" she asks. "We're in the middle of the ocean, miles away from the nearest shore. We're trapped."

The truth of it slams into me. She's right; there is *nowhere* to go. We can't just bail out in a life boat and hope that someone rescues us. But I can't sit here and wait for the worst to happen, either. I have to do something.

At that moment, I hear a commotion on the deck down below. I rush to the window and see dozens of cult members gathered there, their black shirts emblazoned with orange symbols and their faces lit with an unsettling fervor.

They are chanting something, their voices rising like thunder in the air.

I can't make out what they are saying, but the sight of them sends shivers down my spine.

“It has to do with the end times,” Abby says.

My gaze shifts up to the upper deck, and my heart drops when one of the rowdy men from the terminal locks eyes with me. It's like he knows I've been avoiding him—his glare so intense it could incinerate an army of demons. He points at me and then makes a slicing motion across his neck with his finger.

My breath catches as Abby grabs my arm and pulls me away from the window. “We need to stay focused,” she says, her voice shaking. “Like you always say.”

Swallowing hard, I nod in agreement. The situation has gone from bad to worse—not only are we stuck on a ship with dwindling supplies, but there are more than enough shady characters onboard as well.

Abby and I race back to the cabin, me throwing all my weight against the door to double-lock it. We scramble around in the dark, watching news reports and listening to the sounds of the ship creaking and groaning around us. It sounds alive and ready for a fight.

Hours pass, but I can't shake the feeling that someone is out there watching us, waiting for the right moment to strike.

As night falls, the chanting on the deck above us continues to grow louder and more frenzied. Then, just as the first rays of dawn break through the window, we hear a sudden, loud banging at our door. Abby and I leap up in unison, my heart pounding against my chest.

"Who is it?" I call out.

“It's Blake,” comes the reply. “I need to talk to you.”

Fear washes over Abby’s face as we exchange glances. He speaks again with urgency in his voice. “It’s those people,” he says through the door. “The cult. They’ve confiscated all the food.”

16

Passenger 327

The stars glimmer mischievously, like a million pinpricks of light in an infinite black abyss. I sneer up at them and shift my attention to Jenna, who is standing beside me. Her eyes are so dark and mysterious that I can't look away as we enter the cabin. It feels like I have been ensnared in a cryptic trap. She's alluring, and the chanting cultists only heighten this surreal atmosphere. Suddenly, it feels like death is lurking around every corner.

I can only assume this is the reason "Emily" made it so easy for me to bring her here—women on cruise ships don't recognize their own vulnerability. The bright lights and people surrounding them create an illusion of safety and security, but it's no better than meeting a stranger in a dark alley.

Inside, I wait for the pharmaceuticals to take effect, but it appears my companion has a high tolerance. Not high enough not to have killed her friends, but I digress.

We frantically tear off each other's clothes, our skin on fire with anticipation. Her curves shimmer in the moonlight, captivating me with their beauty. Even though I know I'm going to kill her eventually, I can't help but take pleasure in watching her suffer first.

Taking a deep breath, I blurt out, "I have something to confess."

She looks at me with wide-eyed concern.

"I have a wife back home. *Heather*."

Her brows raise. I've touched a nerve, and it's not just because I told her I'm married. Heather—that was Jenna's best friend's name. And Bo, which she thinks is my name, was Heather's brother. Jenna killed them both.

She shrugs, and then slurs her words a bit when she says, "What happens on this ship stays on this ship."

Oh, Jenna. Sweeping things under the rug again. "Yes, but you see, I love Heather. And I don't know what I would do if anything ever happened to her."

"I don't get it. Why would anything happen to her?"

"Who knows? Accidents do happen, don't they, *Jenna*?"

"Who are you?"

"Just call me a family friend."

"I don't believe you."

This time it's me who shrugs. "Believe whatever you want."

Jenna's expression turns dark, and I know she realizes the dangerous game we're playing. But I can't stop myself. I want her to squirm, to feel even a fraction of the pain and fear Heather and Bo went through before they died.

I inch closer to her, breathing in the scent of her skin. "I'm gonna kill you, Jenna Hill," I whisper softly. "But it won't be quick. You will suffer like they did."

She tries to pull away, but my grip is firm.

"You're sick," she hisses.

I laugh—a wild sound that ricochets off the walls caging us in. "You have no idea."

At that moment, I feel a rush of power I have never felt before.

I am in control, and Jenna is at my mercy. I can see the fear in her eyes, and it only makes me want her more.

I shove her back onto the bed, relishing in the way she gasps as I climb on top of her. I know what I'm doing is wrong, but I can't stop myself. It's a sickness—an addiction that I can't resist.

As my hands move over her body, I feel her resistance melting away. She moans and writhes beneath me, and I know she is starting to enjoy herself. But I won't let her forget what's coming.

"You're going to die," I whisper.

The words hang in the air between us, and I can see the fear in Jenna's eyes. But I can also see something else—desire. And I know that if I am careful, I can have her soul in the palm of my hand.

17

Abby

Roger collapses on the sofa after breakfast, murmuring something about resting his eyes, and then he's out cold. We both had a sleepless night, so I decide to let him be—he needs the rest.

Besides, I can get answers faster if he isn't constantly freaking out and holding me hostage in this cabin.

Earlier, this guy Blake came by. He's some sort of computer whiz or something—I don't know the details. Even though Roger is against it—in case he might be infected—he lets Blake hang out for a while. They met in the bar, and now Blake says he can't go back to his cabin because he pissed off one of the cult members and they've confiscated all the food. But Dad says he can't stay here, and Blake says that's fine, he has work to do.

Roger has it in his head that Blake is some sort of undercover journalist, and I can see in Dad's eyes what he's thinking. He thinks Blake can use his contacts to draw attention to our plight and get me off this ship. But when Roger goes into the bathroom, Blake slips out to take a call. That's when I get a look at his laptop screen. A few words jump out at me— like *corporate espionage.*

I'm not up to speed on that kind of thing, but I've seen enough movies to know when something shady is going on. All I know is that whatever Blake is up to, it isn't good. I probably shouldn't say anything else—even if I will be dead soon, I have to think about Roger. Like he's always saying, it's important to know enough, just not too much. That's when things go sideways.

Blake tells Roger we should stick together and Roger kind of agrees, but I think it's a mistake.

Meanwhile, Roger is passed out cold, and Blake is nowhere in sight— thank God for that! He likes to talk, and I have more pressing matters to attend to.

I dress quietly and take off on my own mission to find the boy with the green eyes. I figure, if you can't beat 'em, join 'em, and one thing is for sure: I may be dying, but I am *not* going to starve. If anyone knows anything about the missing food, my bets are on him.

I slip out of the cabin and make my way to deck seven, where I know the cultists like to gather. It's a strange sight, seeing so many people sitting around chanting. I try to blend in, keeping my head down and my eyes averted, but it's hard not to stare. As I suspected, Jacob is here, just as I figured he would be. He's standing at the center of a circle, surrounded by people. Power seems to radiate from him.

I move closer, and he senses me. He turns to look my way, but a boy steps in front of me, blocking my way.

The boy glares at me, and with an angry voice demands, "What do you want?"

"I want to talk about the food situation," I reply without hesitation. "I came to see Jacob."

"Food is for the faithful," he says, narrowing his eyes.

"I want to be faithful," I lie quickly.

He studies me for a moment, then nods. “Very well. But you must prove your devotion first.”

“What do I have to do?”

“Join us in the ritual,” he says, gesturing to the circle.

I don't know what the ritual involves, but I'm determined to find out. I step into the circle, and the cultists close in around me.

"I'm Luke," the boy says. "That over there is our leader, Isaac—"

"I know Isaac."

"*Everyone* knows Isaac." He flashes a grin. "Those are his wives..."

I count six women. “All of them?”

“Yeah—there’s Gina and Letty. And that’s Marla, Birdy, Candace, and that one—her name is Desert Flower.”

A woman parts the crowd and stands beside Isaac's shoulder. “Who's she?”

"Oh, that's Molly Bloom," Luke says. "The new one."

Molly Bloom. It's a name that sounds familiar. But it’s not just the name. She’s the lady from the terminal who almost got Dad killed. I know the harassment wasn’t her fault, but she should have told security the truth when she was questioned. I give her a dirty look.

She stares at me with a mix of curiosity and suspicion but says nothing. The chanting begins, and I try to follow along, but the words are foreign, the meaning lost to me. I feel an odd sensation in the pit of my stomach, like I'm being pulled in two different directions. A voice whispers in my ear, urging me to join them, to let go of my doubts and fears, to embrace the power that flows through the circle. Another voice tells me to run, to get out before it's too late.

"I came to see Jacob," I tell Luke. “I need to get through.”

"I know. But Isaac doesn't let Jacob talk to outsiders."

"Why not?"

"It's complicated."

“Explain it.”

"I can't. But anyway, you shouldn't be here. I know you think we have all the food. That's what Isaac wants everyone to think. But we don't. We only took a little. We don't even have enough for all of us—not even close."

I gaze at him blankly, confused. "So where is it?"

"I can't tell you that," he says, his eyes darting around nervously. "But if you really want to find it, I suggest you go see the old man on deck twelve."

"The old man on deck twelve?"

"Yeah. He's with the crew, I think. He knows things. Maybe he can help you."

I nod, then slip out of the circle and make my way to the old man on deck twelve. When I find him sitting in a corner, his eyes closed, muttering to himself, there is no doubt he's the man Luke was talking about.

"Excuse me," I say, trying to get his attention.

He opens his eyes and looks at me, then smiles. "Hello, child. What can I do for you?"

"I'm looking for food," I answer.

"Ah. I see. The Sons and Daughters of Infinity send you?"

"The who?"

"The cult."

"I was told you were in charge," I say. I'm not sure why, but probably because I think men like hearing that sort of thing.

"God is in charge."

"Yes, but who has the food?"

"They do. But not much. And not for long."

"What do you mean?"

"The end is coming, child. The end of the world. The cult knows it, and they're preparing for it. But they're not the only ones."

"What do you mean?"

"There are others, like me, who know what's coming. And we're preparing too. But our preparations are different. We're not hoarding food or weapons. We're not building bunkers or hiding out in secret rooms. We're doing something else. Something more...spiritual."

"What do you mean?"

He pauses before replying. "We're trying to make contact with something greater than us, something that can lead us out of the bleak future ahead."

He's not making any sense. "You sure you're not with the cult?"

"Well, I'm not *not* with them. Sometimes we just have a difference of opinion. Besides, child, even if it weren't the end times, I don't have many years left. We can't all sit around in the sun chanting. Some of us have to get on with it."

I start to ask what he means, but I've wasted enough time as it is. Roger won't stay asleep forever, and when he wakes, he'll come looking for me.

Then I remember why I'm here—food. "Can you help me find food?"

"I can do better than that, child," he says, his eyes twinkling. "I can help you find salvation."

18

Roger

I jolt awake, my head pounding and my mouth as dry as sandpaper. What the hell happened? I can't remember what day it is, or where I am, or when I fell asleep.

My vision adjusts to the dimly lit stateroom and my eyes dart around, taking in the grandeur of the king-sized bed and elegant furnishings overlooking the endless ocean beyond. It's clear why Abby thought this would be an idyllic vacation— if only it hadn't devolved into an involuntary staycation.

My gaze drops to the clock and a memory suddenly slams into me like a Mack truck. The captain collapsing, the lunatic threatening me, raiding the mini bar after Abby went to sleep, then Blake's incessant banging at daybreak.

Things are slowly beginning to make sense but all I want to do is sleep. There has been no word on the captain's condition yet, but Blake insists that we come up with a plan—he's jumping the gun if you ask me. I need answers about the resources onboard before making any decisions. Stupidity seems to be contagious on this ship, and I decide I would rather not catch it.

I know from my experience in the Army that I need to stay prepared and steer clear of trouble. We have to be careful with whom we align. The company we keep has never been important. Just before leaving, Blake drops his bombshell— he's hacked into the cruise line's computer system and discovers that cultists have raided the storage, taking most of the food reserves.

"What do you mean you hacked the system—so you're not a journalist?"

"I told you," he said. "I work in tech."

"Can you contact the Coast Guard and tell them to send help?"

He looks at me, trying to gauge whether I'm serious. "These people," he says, "they have money. There's a lot of net worth floating around on this ship. If anyone's getting off, I'm guessing it's not going to be you."

What he says makes sense, even if I don't want to hear it. Maybe sticking together isn't the worst plan.

After Blake left, Abby and I ate a meager, room service breakfast in our room, and then I laid down for a nap. When I woke up again, it was noon, and Abby had left me a note saying she'd gone to enjoy some spa treatments. How can they still be giving massages when our captain might be dead and passengers are dropping like flies? What a clown world.

I take solace in a glass of tepid water on the nightstand and finish it in one gulp. Hours have passed since Abby's spa appointment—where is she? I didn't mean to let her go alone, but exhaustion and a killer hangover made me weak.

On shaky feet, I stumble toward the bathroom and relieve myself before splashing cold water onto my face. When I catch my reflection in the mirror, I hardly recognize myself—days without shaving, dark circles under my eyes, pale skin; I'm a wreck.

I take a quick shower and afterward, as I reach for my phone, a sigh escapes when I see there's no service. Perfect. Abby could be trying to call, and I'd never know.

Anxiousness overtakes me as I pick up the phone beside the bed and dial the spa's number.

"Hello," a distant voice answers.

"Hi, I'm looking for Abigail Atkins?"

The attendant informs me that Abby is already in for her facial. It'll be another half hour or so.

I thank her before grabbing my wallet and Abby's meds then head out of the room. Something about being confined is getting to me, and I need some air.

The spa is located at the far end of the ship, and as I wander down a hallway, an altercation erupts from one of the treatment rooms—I hear things being thrown around and raised voices. Then, suddenly, the door flies open to reveal a man in a rage.

"Don't Isaac me!" he yells. "You do as I say! Not the other way around. You hear me, Molly? You fucking hear me?"

He stalks toward me, his eyes seething with hatred. He shakes his head and mutters, "fucking women," then takes off down the hall.

I recognize him instantly—he is one of them; the cult leader, if I'm not mistaken. He strides down the hallway, making a right toward the exit, and I hurry on toward the tearoom where the attendant said Abby would be. But I freeze halfway there when whimpering reaches my ears.

Pressing my eye to a crack in the door, I spy a woman inside. She is wearing nothing but a white towel and her figure takes my breath away—long black hair cascading down her back and legs that seem to go on forever.

As I inch closer for a better look, she turns around and our eyes lock. It's the woman from the terminal. The woman who refused to tell the truth about those guys harassing her. Her expression goes from surprise to shock to fear. Tears are streaming down her cheeks.

“Are you okay?”

She looks so fragile, like a broken bird trying to find its way home. It makes sense now why she wouldn’t report it. She’s used to abuse.

“I’m fine,” she says.

The urge to help her overwhelms me, and I open my mouth to ask if there’s anything I can do or if she'd like me to call somebody, but then I remember it isn't my place to pry. So instead, I quietly inquire again, “Are you sure you’re okay?”

She stares up at me with those big, beautiful eyes and nods silently. Something inside me stirs—a strange feeling that feels oddly familiar all the same. We stand there for what feels like an eternity, lost in each other's gaze, until she finally speaks up. "I never meant for this to happen."

I can't think of anything to say, so I blurt out the first thing that comes to mind. "I'm Roger," I say. "I'm in cabin 217. If you ever need anything—"

"Molly," she instantly stammers back. “I’m Molly.”

Before I can process how to respond, there's a door slamming and then an angry-looking lanky man with dark hair storms down the hall toward us. It's the cult leader coming back. Molly doesn't seem to notice him until it's too late.

"I should never have married him," she whispers, her eyes betraying the terror she feels. "Isaac can be—"

As soon as he sees us standing together, his expression shifts to raw rage, and he stops dead in his tracks. "What the hell is going on here?" he bellows, marching closer. I feel like prey, frozen at the realization a predator is watching me.

He grabs my arm and grips it tightly, growling through his teeth. "Who are you, and why exactly are you in this room with my wife?"

Molly starts to answer, but he silences her with one sharp motion of his hand, ordering her out of the room before things get any worse. His furious eyes burn into me as he waits for an explanation that never comes. He shoves me away and snarls, "If you ever come near either one of us again, there will be consequences."

As Molly turns around, our eyes connect, and she gives me a sad smile.

My heart races as Isaac storms off—I know he'll be keeping an eye on me after this—but despite the danger, my heart still flutters when I look over at the woman standing there with her towel.

19

Passenger 327

They say you never forget your first. And I guess "they" are right since that is exactly who I'm thinking about with Jenna lying beside me.

I remember it like it was yesterday. I watched as the young woman with striking eyes made her way onto the luxury cruise liner. I had heard stories about travelers like her, always searching for something new; she fit the part perfectly. Her excitement was palpable as she moved through the entryway, scanning the faces of fellow passengers with a hint of curiosity and anticipation.

I followed her around the ship and found myself intrigued by her choices. She knew exactly where she was going and wasted no time getting there. I couldn't help being drawn to her, feeling an odd connection I could not explain.

She disappeared into her cabin, and soon after, I heard the sound of shuffling items and running water. A few moments later, a knock at my door startled me out of my thoughts. When I opened it, she was standing there in a light summer dress with a warm smile on her face.

She invited me to check out her cabin. She thought maybe I could "unstick her balcony door."

I asked if I looked like maintenance and she laughed. "I saw you in the hall earlier. It looked like you're traveling alone too?"

"As a matter of fact, I am."

"My cabin is stuffy. And maintenance can take hours. Us loners need to stick together, don't you think?"

I stepped into the cabin and surveyed my surroundings, taking in every detail. There she was: Anna, a delicate creature with an aura of fragility surrounding her like a halo. I could already tell she was going to be more than just another passenger, more than just a brief companion on this voyage. Much more.

My feet quickened as I raced toward her until I stood a mere inch away from her quivering frame. Before she had the chance to react, I seized her in my arms and locked my hands around her fragile neck. Her eyes widened with terror as she desperately fought back against me. But it was futile; I had an iron grip on her, and she knew it.

The darkness began to close in on us, obscuring everything else, until all that remained was a glowing aura that pulsed around us both. I didn't kill her then. Not for days, in fact. We learned a lot about each other in our short time together. Anna was one of a kind. She came from humble beginnings. Pulled herself up by the bootstraps. But that trauma she experienced so early in life? It never left her. She could be cunning. A liar. A thief among thieves. We were a lot alike.

People have said to me, "You don't understand. We only knew each other a week. There's no way they still think about me."

But a person can change your life in a moment. Believe me, it hardly takes a week.

I know because that's what Anna did when she knocked on my door. She invited me into her cabin, into her world.

On the final day of the cruise, as her last breath escaped her lips, so, too, did all the pain, suffering, and heartache that had plagued her life. She would soon journey some place better—far away from the hurt of this world.

I smile at the memory and then I roll over onto my side, staring intently at Jenna, whose wrists are bound and mouth is gagged shut. "Your name isn't Heather, nor is it Jenna. Not anymore. No more games, okay? No more playing around," I mutter sternly.

Tears roll down her porcelain cheeks, which I crudely smear into her skin. "You're Anna now," I whisper. "My darling Anna."

20

Abby

I never do find my salvation. A text message from the spa attendant beeps into my pocket: Roger has called. I slipped her a $20 bill to warn me if he showed up, and she flashed me a smile and said, "Anything else you need, Ms. Atkins?"

Having lived most of my life in sickness, I forget sometimes that things can be so easy.

Now, I'm standing at the window waiting for Roger to get ready for dinner. Tonight, the main restaurant is ours. Food must be getting sparse because they've started rotating who has to use room service and who gets to dine out in one of the three restaurants onboard. It's our turn tonight in the main dining room, and I'm relieved not to have to eat in this cabin once again.

My stomach rumbles as I face an endless horizon. Fear and awe burrow deep within me as I take in the sight of the blue waves below, crashing against the side of the ship and the orange hue of the sunset sky.

A slight chill fills the air, bringing with it the reminder that the world has changed drastically in just a few days.

I try not to think about it. One thing I've learned with my disease is that you can't think too far into the future. With cystic fibrosis, you spend a lot of time literally living from one breath to the next.

My fingertips slide through my hair, and serenity washes over me as I watch the sun slowly dip past the horizon. It's a strange feeling knowing that out there, time is ticking away, but here on the ship, things remain still and small.

I close the curtains, feeling an odd sort of comfort in the familiarity of the cabin. I feel myself beginning to adjust to the fact that we are stuck here for the foreseeable future. The world outside suddenly seems so much larger and scarier.

I flop onto my bed, turn on the nebulizer, and close my eyes. My imagination takes me to a post-apocalyptic world filled with danger, but also possibility and hope.

The ship lurches beneath me, and I'm thrown out of my reverie. My heart thumps like a bass drum as I toss the nebulizer aside and hurry over to the window. But all is quiet; the sea still, just as it was moments ago. Still, an uneasiness lingers in the pit of my stomach.

Shaking off the feeling, I head for the shower to clear my head. I undress and catch a glimpse of myself in the mirror. It's shocking how much weight's melted away since we set sail. My muscles have atrophied and skin clings to bones—I look like a skeleton!

With my eyes shut tight, the steaming shower brings a moment of ease. I drift back in time to when it was all so easy. Last year's memories come flooding back like a torrent. My studies went well, and thankfully, I only spent a few weeks in the hospital over the span of the entire year. Life felt simpler, and with that came contentment.

I knew it couldn't last, and now those days feel like a distant dream. Roger keeps reminding me that it's like this for everyone. Everything has shut down, and no matter what happens when we finally get off this ship, life will not be like it was before.

After the shower, I throw on my best clothes and join Roger in the ship's restaurant for our reservation. The place is packed with passengers, all dressed up and trying to put on a brave face.

We take our seats at a table. Roger orders a drink while I scope out the other passengers, wondering what their stories are. Are they really as happy as they seem? Are they terrified like me?

Before I can say anything to Dad, someone taps his shoulder from behind. He swivels around and finds a woman standing in front of him with a gentle smile. He looks uneasy, almost nervous.

"Mind if I join you?" she asks.

He pauses for a moment before turning back around and nodding. "Yes, please do." He motions to the empty chair next to me.

"You again?" I say with an eye roll.

The woman takes a seat and introduces herself as Molly—as though I don't know who she is. I think she means for her warm smile and kind eyes to reassure me, but they don't.

I observe my dad and Molly together, and I swear Roger is flirting! I don't know what he's thinking. This isn't the sort of distraction we need right now.

The ship lurches violently, throwing me and Molly into each other. The lights flicker on and off, sparking a wave of fear through the restaurant. It stops just as suddenly as it began.

"What was that?" Molly gasps. I'm about to answer her when the captain's voice booms from the loudspeaker. His tone is measured, yet chillingly calm.

"Attention all passengers, this is your captain speaking. We are experiencing technical difficulties, but everything is under control. Please return to your normal activities."

I turn to Dad, my words barely a whisper in the tension-filled air. "But I thought the captain was dead."

Molly shakes her head. She grips the armrests so hard her knuckles turn white. "Guess we got a new one."

21

Roger

The hairs on my neck stand up as Molly's intense gaze meets mine across the deck. I've been waiting for her to arrive, and now that she's here, I understand why I am so nervous. Her long gray dress holds her slender frame like a cocoon and a delicate veil covers her face—likely to conceal her identity. She's stunning.

My heart races as I keep my eyes fixed on hers until she glides gracefully toward the table and sits down. The air crackles with electricity before we even speak.

Blake had broken the news to me over breakfast: Molly, a former farm girl from Iowa, was now married to Isaac the Enlightened—the infamous cult leader onboard who is well known for his brutality.

At dinner, she'd pressed a slip of paper into my hand, and now I'm drawn to this secluded deck she requested to meet on. She sits back against a low railing, pale light playing in her dark hair, and I feel my stomach tighten with something more than curiosity.

"Hello," Molly whispers in a voice that sounds like velvet and honey combined.

I respond in kind with my own soft whisper. "Hello."

I'm desperate to look away but can't seem to tear my gaze from her captivating beauty.

We stay silent for a few moments until finally Molly leans in closer and speaks in a low sultry voice — sending shivers through my body.

"Thank you for meeting me tonight," she says. "I know it was a lot to ask."

"What do you mean?" I say, clearing my throat.

"It's risky," Molly confirms what I already know. "But I'm sure you understand."

Her words hang between us, potent with an unspoken understanding that our meeting is something more than a simple conversation.

I nod slowly, my heart pounding even faster. "I had to see you," she murmurs. "I needed to speak to someone who isn't part of our...group."

My eyes sweep the area, making sure no one is watching. "What's going on?"

She takes a deep breath, and then exhales slowly, as though she's rehearsed what she's about to say. "I need your help. I'm scared, and I don't know who to trust. Isaac is... he's not what he seems."

I raise an eyebrow, intrigued. "What do you mean? What's he done?"

Molly hesitates, biting her lip. "He's...he's been hurting people. Members who disobey him. And I think he's...I think he's planning something terrible. Something big."

My heart sinks as the gravity of the situation hits me. I try to keep my face neutral, but inside I'm reeling. "What do you need from me?"

"I don't know..."

"You don't know?" I repeat. "You must have some idea. You took a risk just to meet me."

"What he's planning, Roger—a lot of people will be hurt."

"That's... that's insane." I lean in closer, trying to hide the urgency in my voice. "How?"

She delves into her dress pocket and pulls out a folded sheet of paper. "This is the plan. I managed to steal it from Isaac's cabin. I need you to get it to the authorities when we dock in the next port. If he finds me with this—if he finds out I've said anything to *anyone*—I'm dead, Roger. Do you understand?"

I take the paper from her and unfold it, quickly skimming its contents. It's a comprehensive plan for a mass suicide—complete with step-by-step instructions on how to carry it out.

My stomach turns at the thought. "How many people are involved?"

"I don't know for sure, but I think most members are in on it. They believe they're going to a higher plane of existence or something like that."

I shake my head, trying to clear it. "Fuck."

"I know."

Tucked into the paper is a key card. "What's this?"

"It's universal; it'll get you into any room on this ship. Just in case."

I look out over the water and finally back at her. "Okay," I say. "I'll take this plan to the captain—to security. But what about you, Molly? You can't stay with him if he's hurting people."

"I know," she whispers, tears streaming down her face. "But I have nowhere else to go. He made sure of that. He'd kill me if I tried to leave—he's killed others for much less than that."

Reaching out, I take her hand and give it a gentle squeeze. "Don't worry—we'll figure something out."

She looks up at me with gratitude in her eyes. "Thank you. I knew I could trust you."

We sit in silence for a few moments, lost in our own thoughts. The ship rocks gently beneath us, the only sound the distant hum of the engines.

Suddenly, Molly stands up, pulling her veil back over her face. "I have to go. He'll be looking for me."

22

Abby

I step onto deck eight, my heart pounding with anticipation. This is it. I'd worked up the courage to sneak away and meet a boy I barely know—a boy with green eyes who captivates me.

Not that it was difficult to sneak out—Roger is who-knows-where, meeting Blake to come up with some sort of "plan."

The thumping music from the nightclub reverberates through the still air as I make my way across the ship. The salt-infused ocean breeze fills me with energy, pushing aside the doubts that threaten to steal away my nerves.

When I reach the brightly lit club, he's already there—at the bar, nursing a drink. Our eyes lock, and my heart leaps wildly. He smiles, and something inside me shifts and changes. A spark of possibility, an awakening of my own desires, fills me like never before.

He found me in the spa yesterday and invited me here tonight.

When I asked how he'd known I would be at the spa, he told me "his people" have eyes everywhere.

"The club is where passengers our age hang out," he'd said. He told me he had something he wanted to talk to me about. Something important. So here I am.

"So what's your deal?" he asks as I casually stroll up to the bar.

"What's my deal?" I reply cautiously.

"I mean, what's with the oxygen? You have cancer or something?"

My mouth goes dry as I stutter an answer. "No...CF."

"What's CF?" he asks innocently.

"Cystic fibrosis."

A darkening of his expression follows as he peers into my eyes. "Oh. How long have you been sick?" His voice is gentle yet heavy with concern.

"I can't remember ever not having CF."

"What's it like? I'm sorry—it's just I've never heard of it..."

"It's brutal."

"How so?"

I struggle to keep my voice steady as emotion tightens around my throat like a vise's grip. "Last time I was in the hospital, it felt like my body wasn't even mine anymore. The doctors say I won't make it to eighteen. The last one said that my lungs are so bad the next bout of pneumonia would probably be the one that kills me."

Jacob stares back at me, his eyes wide in shock. "Wow," he says. "I don't know what to say..."

"Sometimes there is nothing to say."

"That sucks."

I nod grimly. "It isn't easy—managing my meds, tracking my breathing, staying healthy with everything working against me... but it is what it is." I shrug. "You get used to it."

His eyes blaze with sudden determination as he reaches out his hand, and my cheeks flush in response. "I asked you here because I like you, Abby."

My mouth falls open. I don't know what I was expecting him to say, but I never imagined he'd be so blunt.

Jacob hesitates for a moment before speaking. "And I want you to know that whatever happens—it's not personal."

"What does that mean?" I cock my head. "Is this about the food?"

"Sort of. Look—he's been talking about a new world order for as long as I can remember. Says he wants to create a society where only the strongest survive. I guess that's sort of how we ended up here. Anyway— he's been stockpiling supplies, and he's been training his followers to fight. I wouldn't want to be on the other side if I were you."

"Who's *he*? Isaac?"

His eyes flit toward the door then land back on me. "Who else?"

"I heard that starting tomorrow we all have to collect our rations on deck. No more room service and no more dining out."

I expect this to be news to Jacob, but it isn't

I do a double-take. "You already knew?"

"I told you. I know people. Crew or whatever."

I think of my mother. I consider asking Jacob if he can find out anything about her, but I don't want to come across like I'm using him, like I want something from him. "What about the captain?" I say. "Is he really dead?"

Jacob shrugs. "How should I know?"

"And the 'technical difficulties'—I guess you don't know about those either?"

"I'd tell you, but then I'd have to kill you."

A corner of my mouth curls up. "I'm dying anyway—might as well get it over with."

He smirks as he pulls me close. "I'm only kidding—but you're funny, you know that?"

"I—" The words *Morgan Atkins* and *please help me find my mother* almost roll off my lips, but then he leans in and I can smell his aftershave, and I can't force myself to say them.

"Dance with me," he whispers into my ear.

"Here?"

"Sure. Why not?"

He draws me closer, and we sway together in perfect harmony, saying more than words ever could. His hands remain firm yet gentle on my waist while his thumb circles small patterns across my spine, sending warmth radiating through my body and leaving me feeling safe in his embrace.

"I like you," he tells me again. "Which is why I want you on our side."

"I didn't know there *were* sides."

"You speak like you don't know what's going on."

"I don't."

"We've taken most of the food—what we could get our hands on, anyway. Isaac is serious about his plans. Everyone is."

"So, what?" I pull back and search his face. "I join you and then what?"

"Then you don't have to worry."

I laugh. I can't help myself. "You don't know what it's like to be me."

I inch up onto my toes and peer into his eyes. There is something new in his expression, a certain sadness. His lips curl into half a smile as if he knows what I'm thinking, and suddenly any trace of fear evaporates. "You're right. You want a drink?"

"I'm only sixteen."

"So? I'm seventeen," he says. "Come on, I know the bartender."

"I don't drink, actually. Can't mix my meds and liquor—you know all that jazz."

He takes my hand in his and intertwines our fingers. "Fine, but come with me anyway."

"Why me?" I blurt out.

"What?"

“Why do you want—” I pause and force air into my lungs. “Why do you want me on your side. I mean, look at me.”

“Simple,” he says. “Isaac told me a year ago I’d meet a girl who was sick. He said we’d journey to the afterlife together.”

“That sounds crazy.”

Jacob smiles. “Come on, it’ll sound less crazy after a drink.”

I shift on my heel and run smack into my dad, his face grim and determined. "Abby, what the hell?" he says, and when he leads me away, I let him. But not before I glance back at the boy, wondering what might have been if I’d stayed.

23

Passenger 327

I stand at the window of my cabin, watching the ship slice through the waves, and reflect on the impossibility of speaking to a caterpillar in butterfly language. A vicious thrill courses through me as I realize I'm both powerful and powerless at the same time.

Jenna's behavior has been out of control since this morning—I know it's a sign that drastic measures must be taken soon. Then comes the announcement over the loudspeaker that food rationing will be implemented due to broken freezers—a total lie. Everyone knows who is really responsible for stealing the food, but no one wants to call them out and face the consequences.

Appearances must be kept, after all.

Jenna cowers in the corner of my cabin, contorting her battered body to find some relief from the aching pain that engulfs her. Bruises cover every inch of her visible flesh, barely allowing her to move. She whimpers softly, a low hum that makes me want to laugh at her misery. I can't control myself—the announcement brings with it an imminent dread. How am I supposed to be with her and go collect rations at the same time? Eventually, the drugs will run out. This means I need a heartier solution—and fast.

Rumors swirl through the air as everyone hears about a possible engine malfunction. When I relay the news to Jenna, terror flashes across her face as she realizes there is no escape. Her fear makes me temporarily forget about my little problem with the diminishing medication. It feeds a satisfaction inside me that surpasses anything else. *The strongest steel is made in the hottest fire.*

I watch her closely, suppressed laughter rising up inside me at the thought of my plan coming together perfectly. The control I feel is unlike anything else; it is power, pure and simple.

You might be thinking: why go to all this trouble? And I understand what you mean. I do not usually "keep" my victims, but every once in a while I come upon someone truly worthy. Like Anna, and now Jenna.

I realize it will not be easy to morph Jenna into Anna. But nothing good in life ever comes easy. Not even *Anna* became Anna overnight. I molded her into the perfect woman, same as I will Jenna.

The captain keeps blathering over the loudspeaker, but he stops mentioning the food rationing that has become necessary. He seems determined to keep things as normal as possible, though his words do nothing to calm anyone down.

I savor every second, plotting how I'll keep Jenna under my control and imagining how she'll look in the end. Nothing will stop me.

The passengers are growing increasingly anxious and desperate. On top of wondering how long they'll be stuck on this ship, they now have to worry about what will happen when we reach our destination. I also find myself wondering what will happen when we can finally disembark. Will I be able to keep Jenna a secret until then, or will someone discover her whereabouts? I'm not sure, but I am determined to see my plan through.

Days slip past, and the rationing continues, eating away at the passengers' sanity. Some cling to hope while others crack under the pressure. All the while, I keep watch over Jenna, slowly breaking her down, transforming her into everything I know she can be.

24

Roger

Last night we docked to refuel, but no one was allowed to enter or exit the ship. There is said to be a measles outbreak in the country, though whether that was true or just an excuse to keep us onboard remains to be seen.

Anyone who tried to disembark was notified they would be immediately arrested, and I guess no one was brave enough to volunteer for prison in a third world country—especially not one with a measles outbreak. Not even me. We were all ordered to remain in our cabins as the ship was refueled and supplies were loaded. Most of us listened.

But that changes once we leave port. Once we've moved further out to sea, Blake and I step out of my cabin and make our way onto the cruise ship's main deck. It is nearly empty, as most of the passengers have retired for the night, but the upper deck is still alive with activity. The sound of shouting from above is growing louder and more chaotic as the crew attempts to contain the chaos emerging from above.

Blake looks at me with wide eyes. “What's going on?”

I shake my head. "I'm not sure, but it doesn't sound good."

"Should we go back to the cabin?" he asks, glancing around nervously.

"No," I say. "We should stay and find out what's happening."

I step forward, craning my neck to look at the upper deck. “It doesn’t look good.”

“You think pirates boarded while we were in port? I’ve heard stories… We need to arm ourselves somehow.”

“We can hardly get food—how do you think we’re going to get a gun?”

Blake looks at me and shakes his head. “The internet, how else?”

“We don’t have the internet anymore—and even if we did—what are they going to do, drop it by drone?”

“Why not?”

Suddenly, a figure emerges from the shadows. Blake gasps and steps back, but I recognize her immediately.

"Molly!" I exclaim. "What in the hell is going on?"

She smiles, but her expression is distant. "Roger?” she says. "What are you two doing here?"

Blake hesitates before answering. "We're trying to figure out what's going on."

Molly nods gravely. "It's been crazy." Her eyes scan the area and then she leans forward and whispers, "Something strange is happening on the ship. I think someone is trying to seize control."

“Who?” I take a step toward her. “I mean, how do you know?”

Molly stares at me with a serious expression. “I don’t know for sure, but I think they’re attempting a coup.”

Blake and I exchange worried glances. "What should we do?" Blake asks quietly.

Molly shakes her head. "I don't know—but, if I were you, I wouldn't trust anyone."

Blake stares at her. "What do you mean?"

I run my hand across my jaw and look at Molly. "Where are we headed?"

She sighs. "I don't know."

"You don't know or you won't say?" Blake asks.

"Isaac is very selective about the information he shares and with whom he shares it. I can't tell you everything, because I don't *know* everything. Just be careful."

A loud announcement blares over the speakers as if on cue.

"Attention passengers, due to a recent incident, strict curfews will now be enforced. We are headed back to Miami. Please report to deck five at your respective times to receive your meals and return directly to your cabins until further notice."

Molly looks us straight in the eyes. "You should stay away from deck five," she warns gravely. "It could be dangerous."

"What should we do then?" Blake says, his voice barely audible above the din of the repeating announcement.

Molly mulls it over for a few moments before responding, "Stay away from Isaac and his followers," she says. "And keep your eyes open. Whatever it is they're up to, you don't want to be caught in the middle of it."

"This is his plan?" I demand, pivoting toward Molly, and Blake seems to stiffen.

He gives both of us a tentative look before inquiring, "What plan?"

Molly and I reply in a robotic unison, "Nothing."

There's a certain look of understanding on Blake's face, though it's overshadowed by doubt.

Molly motions for us to follow. "We'd better duck into the restroom so we can talk privately," she whispers.

We creep down the hallway, looking out for any of Isaac's

followers. Once inside, Molly checks the stalls before speaking again.

"Remember," she says. "No matter what you hear, don't trust anyone. Isaac's men are up to something, and you don't want to be involved."

"You're his wife," Blake says, raising an eyebrow. "Why are you telling us this?"

Molly's face hardens. "Because no one else is going to," she snaps. "And just because I'm married to him doesn't mean I agree with everything he does."

"Is he really killing people?" Blake asks. "All the deaths— is it the virus or is it *him*?"

Molly sighs and looks away. "I can't speak to that."

"What was the point of dragging us in here, then?" Blake asks with an eye roll. "If you can't tell us anything—"

"Listen—I have to go. Isaac's waiting for me. But if I were you, I'd stay out of sight—stay in your cabins. I'm sorry," she says. "That's really all I can tell you."

I nod, and with that, Molly disappears into the darkness of the corridor.

The next morning, Abby and I wake to news of another death onboard the ship. It seems the cult has taken control, and they are now enforcing their own rules. Rations are being strictly enforced, and curfews are being imposed. Rumor has it the cult killed our former captain and installed their own guy. This way there will be no issues with the authorities. They haven't even been alerted. Along with the freezers, cell service and Wi-Fi remain inoperable as well.

The inability to communicate with the outside world forces passengers to face the seriousness of the situation, and panic spreads.

Later that night, as we are getting ready for bed, there is a loud knock on the cabin door. Abby and I freeze, as if we know something is coming.

The door swings open, and there stand two of Isaac's henchman, with the cult leader himself between them. "We know what you're up to," Isaac growls. "You're conspiring against us. We know, and we won't stand for it. You will be punished."

Abby and I remain silent, terror freezing us in place. Isaac continues, "You will be taken to the brig, where you will be held until further notice. I suggest you keep your mouth shut and cooperate if you wish to avoid further repercussions."

The two cult members grab me and drag me out of the cabin. I am taken to the brig, a steel room which is located on one of the bottom decks of the vessel, near the security office. When they lock me in a room where I am forced to wait, I see no sign of security. Have they killed them all? Am I next? I don’t know what is going to happen to me, but I know one thing: My daughter needs me, and I have to get out of here. I have to escape.

25

Passenger 327

It is my darkest hour; Jenna's behavior leaves a lot to be desired, and also I have been tracking my target through the labyrinthine corridors of the ship. For hours, I have been lurking in the shadows, patiently stalking my prey. I have become a master of disguise, a ghost among the living, undetected and undeterred in my mission.

Finally, my patience pays off.

I stand in the darkness, watching as my victim exits the elevator and makes her way down the corridor. I hiss menacingly as she passes; a warning and a promise of what is coming. She quickens her pace, her eyes darting from side to side as she tries in vain to spot her pursuer.

But it is too late.

I emerge from the darkness and force the woman into her cabin. She shrieks in terror as I advance, my hands like iron claws, tightly gripping her shoulders. I push her inside and close the door behind us.

She begs for mercy, but I have none to offer. I wrap my hands around her neck, strangling her until she is still.

When the deed is done, I take a moment to catch my breath and survey the scene. There is a chair tipped over beside the bed, a pair of slippers on the floor. The woman has been preparing for the night, thinking only of her own comfort.

Now, she is dead.

I make my way back out of the cabin and through the long corridors of the ship. I retrieve a wheelchair from outside a room, push it back to the cabin, and after a few moments of difficulty, I manage to maneuver her body into it.

I wheel her through the ship, her corpse slumped in the chair, a grotesque parody of the living. Along the way, I pretend she has merely passed out. I offer polite smiles and mutter good evenings to the other passengers. They give me knowing looks. Alcohol is the one thing that is still flowing freely on this ship.

Finally, I reach my cabin. I open the door and see Jenna lying on the bed. She stirs, blinking awake to the sight of the dead woman being wheeled in.

I give her a menacing look, a warning not to try to speak through her gag. Then I gesture to the corpse and say, "Your job is to bathe her, dress her, and make her presentable. Do it quickly, and do it well."

I fetch a washcloth from the bathroom, then Jenna's brushes and makeup case. She stares at me in horror but remains silent. I untie her gag and instruct her on how to gently wash the woman's face. A smirk crosses my lips as Jenna tries to smooth away all traces of terror from the woman's features.

She trembles as she wipes away moisture and blood, then applies makeup to her cheeks and eyes.

I retrieve one of Jenna's dresses from her luggage. "That's my favorite one," Jenna protests.

"Anna always loved helping the needy," I reply, amused. "You'll learn."

I help a reluctant Jenna as she dresses the corpse. When she is finished, the woman lies in the bed, her features peaceful in death. She looks almost serene, like a sleeping angel.

I stand and give a satisfied nod.

Then I tug her lifeless body closer to Jenna's side of the bed, retie Jenna's restraints, and together we whisper a prayer for the woman's soul before I cover her with a sheet to her chin.

"I'll find a proper resting place for her," I say to Jenna, "when you learn to behave."

She closes her eyes and tears stream down her cheeks. "Oh, Anna, darling," I say. "Don't cry. Fate can be fickle; this could just as easily have been your destiny."

26

Abby

I stand on the deck of the ship, my wind-tousled hair blowing in the salty sea breeze. I scan the horizon, my gaze cutting through the endless blue expanse of the ocean. I left the safety of my cabin only moments ago, granted this half hour of outside privileges by the Sons and Daughters of Infinity, the elusive new leaders of this vessel.

It has been two days since they dragged Dad away from our cabin. I haven't seen him since, not even a glimpse. Anxiety crawls up my throat, tightening around my windpipe, and I push it away. Dad would say to focus on the present moment. Although I fear the worst, I know he's right. Dwelling on what might be happening to him will only cloud my judgment.

I make my way back to the cabin, my steps heavy with dread. I pause at the door, hesitating before I open it. Our room feels cold and empty without Dad here. There is no laughter bubbling up from the room anymore, no card games or jokes or stories to keep me distracted. A few items still lay where he left them when they dragged him away. I know nothing can be changed by staying outside, but perhaps I can stay here in the hall for just a few more minutes.

"Any luck?"

I turn at the sound of the voice. It's Blake. He is tall and handsome, with dark brown eyes and a ready smile. He has become a trusted friend over the last few days, and I am grateful for his kindness.

"No," I say. "I was just...praying."

Blake gives me a sympathetic smile. "I know. I'm sure he's okay. They have to be treating him well."

My hands shake. I clasp them behind my back so that Blake won't see. My fingers twine with each other, nervous and impatient and scared, like they have a mind of their own.

"I hope you're right."

Blake nods. He reaches out and touches my arm gently. "Hey, you want to come with me to deck five? I heard they're handing out fresh bread."

I shake my head. "No, thanks. I should get back."

"Okay. Well, if you need anything, just let me know."

I offer a sad smile. "Thanks, Blake."

"Just hang tight, okay?"

"What other choice do I have?"

He nods, and then he is gone. I watch him disappear down the hallway until he is just a speck in the distance.

I open the door to my cabin and step inside. Molly is standing there. She wears a pained expression on her face, her eyes wide with worry.

I don't mean to freak out, but the sight of her leaves me with zero chill. I fear the worst. *Why else would she have come?* "Is he okay? Did they let him go?"

She shakes her head. "Not yet."

My eyes narrow. "How'd you get in here?"

"It doesn't matter," she says impatiently. "I wanted to check on you."

Her words are rushed, frantic, as if she has been waiting for hours for me to return.

"I also want to let you know he's okay," she says quickly. "They're just questioning him. It's taking a little longer than expected." She pauses for a moment before adding, "I know this isn't what you wanted to hear, and I'm sorry."

I know what she means—she is sorry for getting Roger into this mess—but her apology is pointless. I am seething with rage. She had no right to drag him into this bloody game, and yet I can't find the words to convey my anger. I can only feel a dull ache in my chest as the world seems to crumble around me.

The other issue—I don't want to burn any bridges. I realize Molly might be the only person who can help him.

"Do you need anything?" she asks tentatively, as if expecting me to yell at her or push away her offer of help.

"No," I say bitterly. "Not from you."

Molly nods before turning to leave the room. As she walks away, I feel an overwhelming sense of sadness wash over me, like an ocean wave crashing onto shore—all of our hopes and dreams swallowed up in its wake.

27

Roger

The cult marches me through the bowels of the cruise ship, the cold steel of the handcuffs biting into my wrists. Every step feels like a lurch toward my fate, and I can feel their eyes boring into me like laser beams. There are no words spoken, no questions asked. My captors are resolute in their mission, and their grip is so tight and merciless that I can barely lift my arms.

I stumble, and they yank me forward, a chill running through me as I realize what's happening. There's only oppressive darkness and silence—except for the relentless beat of my heart. I'm a prisoner of fanatics, with no clue about my future. Every step takes me closer to the unknown, dread filling my veins at what might be waiting for me at the end.

The corridor is narrow and dark, flashing red emergency lights flickering and buzzing above me. There's a muted roar of the sea and a shrill creaking of the ship's hull, and a low hum of electricity. The cult members march me along until we reach a heavy steel door with a small window set in it. One of them produces a key, unlocking it before throwing it open.

"Welcome to your new residence," he sneers, pushing me inside the small cell. I stagger in, feeling my stomach plummet as I hear the door slam shut behind me with a loud clang.

The room is nothing more than a tiny box of metal walls, barely bigger than my body. It reeks of urine and sweat. There is no furniture, no windows; just one bare bulb hanging from the ceiling that casts an eerie light across my prison cell. A thick blanket lies crumpled in one corner, giving off an unbearable musty smell that makes my stomach turn over in revulsion.

I sink to my knees on the cold floor out of sheer exhaustion, my wrists still tightly bound behind my back. I feel powerless against these people; this cult has effectively taken away all control I have over my life and holds me captive in their world, where I am nothing more than a pawn in their game.

A muffled voice from outside interrupts my thoughts, calling out orders in cryptic words that make little sense to me, but it is clear from the tone that they mean business. They want something from me—something they think I have—but what? All I can do now is wait until they reveal their next move...

I sit slumped on the floor, trembling, feeling as if I am about to be swallowed up by the darkness. Suddenly, the door swings open, and a man in a hood drags me from the cell. He marches me to a larger room where a group of men in hoods wait. I am dragged to the center of the room. They circle around me, their eyes glittering with hatred.

My heart feels like it's going to pound out of my chest as I stare up at the hooded men that fill the room. Despite the hoods, I can see they are young—younger than me by far. Men in their prime: powerful, dangerous-looking figures. There is no escape from them.

As they circle me like vultures, my mind races with questions. *What do they want from me? Do they really expect me to answer their questions honestly? Are these people even human or something else entirely?*

A bulky man strides forward and speaks in a low, menacing voice.

"We have questions for you, Roger," he says. "You must answer us truthfully, or the consequences will be more severe than you can fathom." His words send a shudder of fear through my body.

One of the cult members takes out a sharp knife and presses it against my neck, his eyes glaring into mine with a sinister gleam.

"Answer our questions," he growls, pressing harder and making me gasp in pain. “Or you die.”

The other men stand around watching silently, as if waiting for some kind of signal from the one holding the knife.

“You wrote a manifesto and tried to pin it on our leader, no?”

When I manage to speak, I stammer. “I…don’t know…I don’t know anything about any manifesto.”

The man takes a fist full of my hair and rips what he can out at the roots. “You are a liar!” He punches me several times. “You will answer us truthfully this time, yes?”

I close my eyes and try to focus on staying calm despite the fear building inside me. As hard as it is, I know I have to stay strong in order to get out of this situation alive. Taking a deep breath, I open my eyes and meet each of their gazes before answering solemnly, "Yes—I’ll answer your questions truthfully."

The heavy-set man nods slowly before continuing. He asks several pointed questions about my beliefs and past actions, but nothing that makes me feel like I'm in any immediate danger—just an interrogation to try to get information out of me. But then he shifts direction. He wants to know about my encounter with Molly in the spa.

The man grows angry, and I shudder as he holds the knife up

in front of my face. He asks me questions about other passengers, other members of the cult, and their activities, but I cannot answer them. I can only stare in fear, feeling the blade pressing against my neck.

I want to tell him about Abby—that she's sick, and she needs me. But I do not want to draw attention to her. I don't want to give them a reason to go back to that cabin. I do not want them to question her as they are me.

The man presses the knife harder against my skin, and a trickle of blood runs down my neck. The other cultists hold me down, and I feel nausea washing over me.

Finally, the man steps back, satisfied. After a while, the men all leave, their footsteps echoing down the corridor. I lie on the floor, exhausted and trembling. My body aches from the beatings, and blood is trickling down my neck from the knife blade.

I lay there for what feels like an eternity, trying to make sense of what's happening. I am terrified by the cultists' interrogation, and it seems like they will never give up on trying to get information from me.

At some point, I lose consciousness, and when I wake, I am back in the smaller cell. I do not know how long I have been here. Hours, days, weeks—it all merges in a blur of pain and terror. They come for me often; they question me relentlessly, torturing me with their blades, their fists, their threats. But I never give in. I never give them the answers they want. How can I? I don't have them.

My days and nights become a blend of pain, despair, and terror. With no end in sight, hope is drifting away that I will ever get out of this living hell.

I think about Abby, about how she needs me to survive down here, how her life depends on it—and that feeling keeps me going through each new day of torture.

But despite my resilience, every day is a struggle to stay alive.

At times, it feels like death would be a welcome relief from the relentless pain and suffering. But then I remember my promise to Abby—that I would always be there for her—and it gives me the courage to keep fighting.

28

Abby

I step up to Blake's cabin door and knock, my heart pounding in my chest. I'm desperate for his help—it's like the saying goes: the most obvious answer is usually the correct one, except it wasn't obvious until this morning.

"Just a minute," comes a gruff voice from inside the cabin. Several loud thumps echo off the walls on the other side. The door slowly creaks open, revealing a scowling Blake, looking like he hasn't slept in days, his hair is a wild mess. It feels like he's aged ten years overnight.

"Abby?" he exclaims. "What are you doing here?"

I close my eyes and take a long breath, steadying myself before I speak. My words come out faster than I want them to. "I need your help. I'm looking for information on my mother and was hoping you could hack into the ship's records."

Blake's expression softens, and then he nods with understanding. "I can try," he says. "But it won't be easy. The security on those records is top-notch. And I can't get online—at least not yet; I'm working on it. But I can look at what I have."

Relief floods through me, and I let out a sigh. "Thank you."

I shift from foot to foot. "Oh, and I was wondering—what about the security cameras?"

"What about them?"

"I was thinking you could take a look and see where they took my dad..."

"Hmmm. Tell you what," Blake says with a nod of his head. "Let me wash up and get dressed and I'll meet you back at your cabin in twenty or so?"

"Sure," I reply without hesitation, already feeling better about our odds of success now that Blake is helping me out.

My next stop is deck seven. I know I have to be careful. The cult has spies everywhere, and I don't want to draw attention to myself.

I search desperately for Jacob, praying he can help me get my father out of captivity. At the very least, he might be able to get messages back and forth.

I find him in a restaurant that should be closed, but instead it's bustling with cult members. He is sitting at a table, talking to a couple of other young men. His eyes narrow when he sees me, and I sense his guardedness. He stands from the table, and I follow him to the other side of the room.

"Jacob," I say breathlessly, my voice trembling. "I need your help."

Recognition flashes in his eyes as he looks me up and down. "Abby, you shouldn't be here."

"I know," I say, trying to keep my voice low. "And I'm sorry. But I didn't know what else to do. I need to get my father out of wherever it is they're keeping him."

Something dark passes across Jacob's face, and he shakes his head. "I'm afraid I can't help you with that."

My desperation rises and I plead, "Why not?"

He refuses to meet my gaze. “It's complicated.”

"I don't care," I say, my voice rising. "I need to know what's going on. I need to help my father."

Jacob leans in closer. "Listen to me, Abby," he instructs in a low rasp. "This isn't just about your father. There are bigger things at play here—things you wouldn't understand."

I lift my chin defiantly. "Try me.”

Jacob stares at me, like he can see right through me, before finally giving a nod. "All right," he agrees reluctantly, "but you have to promise me you won't tell anyone what I'm about to tell you. And I mean *no* one."

"Okay," I agree, my heart racing with anticipation.

Jacob inhales sharply, and the words seem to catch in his throat. "This cult isn't what you think," he says. "They're not about enlightenment or spiritual growth. It's about them keeping their power by any means necessary—even if it means hurting people."

My vision blurs as oxygen seems to be sucked from the air around me, but I check my battery oxygen concentrator—it’s fine. “Tell me something I don’t know.”

“I don’t think you get it. What I mean is,” he says in an icy whisper, “there are experiments being conducted on this ship. Experiments that involve human subjects. And your father is one of them.”

My heart drops into my stomach. "What kind of experiments?" I manage to force out past the lump in my throat.

"I don't know all the details," Jacob admits. "But I do know they're doing it all in secret, hidden away in a part of the ship that even I don't have access to."

I feel like I've been punched in the gut. All this time, my father has been suffering, and there's nothing I can do.

"How can I get him out?" I plead.

“I don't know,” Jacob replies. “But we need to be careful—if anyone finds out we're talking about this, we'll both be toast. Got it?”

"I understand," I say quickly, already plotting ways in which we might free him. "I'll be careful. But what else would we be talking about?"

"Exactly. That's why I need you to stay away—I don't want to be implicated."

"Fine."

As I turn to leave, Jacob reaches out and grabs my arm. "Abby, I'm serious. It'll be bad news if I'm seen talking to you again—especially if it's one of the leaders. The people behind this aren't the kind who mess around."

I contemplate my next move and reply, "You're right. I shouldn't have come."

"I'm sorry, but this has to happen." He gives me a sad smile and then and puts one finger to his lips. With a raised voice he says, "Don't ever fucking come here again! You hear? I have nothing else to say to you!"

Tears sting my eyes. "Jacob—please?" I choke out.

He shakes his head while backing away. "Please? Seriously? You had the chance—we tried to welcome you in—you made your choice!"

I burst into tears and hurry out. I don't mean to cry, but it's clear how bad the situation is. I check the battery on my concentrator. I have one more stop to make before meeting Blake, and hopefully just enough battery to do it. Admittedly, I have not been keeping up with things the way Roger did. It's strange, I guess I never really realized just *how* much he does for me. I mean, I *thought* I knew. But I didn't *know.*

When I round the corner and step into the hallway, Molly is standing there holding a bundled sandwich. She takes me by my shirtsleeve and pulls me into a stairwell.

"I heard you were looking for Jacob," she says. "I thought you might be hungry."

I nod, my heart racing. I can't trust her, but I appreciate the gesture. "Thank you," I say, taking the sandwich.

Molly looks uneasy and keeps glancing around like she's worried about someone seeing us together. "This was a bad idea," she says. "I need to keep a low profile, and I recommend you do the same. But I just wanted you to know," she whispers, her voice heavy with emotion, "that I'm working on getting your dad free. I haven't given up."

I wipe my face with the back of my hand and take a deep breath. Then I straighten my back, fighting back the urge to let myself fall apart completely. Instead, I simply nod and say, "I appreciate that. But I really wish you'd try a little harder."

"I know." She reaches out and squeezes my arm before walking away without another word.

29

Roger

My wrists burn as the ropes dig into my skin, blood trickling down my arms. Gagged and tossed into a black abyss with no way out. It feels like I've been here forever. Why me? What have I done to deserve this?

The three lead interrogators are younger this time. One looks familiar—Abby's date from that night at the nightclub.

Finally, Isaac strolls in. It's the first time I've seen him since my captivity. He prefers others to do his dirty work for him.

"Welcome to the grand experiment," he sneers. He crouches down to get a better look at me. "You see, we must teach our brothers and sisters a lesson: It is unacceptable to be disloyal to the Sons and Daughters of Infinity."

"We must show them how to bear pain, just like you," he continues. "But more than that, we must instruct them on how to inflict suffering when needed—the same way a father disciplines his child when they misbehave, you understand?"

"Just kill me and get it over with," I murmur. I'm too exhausted to rebel or find something clever to say to make them finish me off already.

They keep asking the same questions, but I stay true to my answers and refuse to break. Yet their rage grows clearer with each passing second; it's plastered across their faces.

My eyes dart around the room, searching for any escape route. But there is none—my captors have me cornered. Fear courses through my veins like lightning as they raise the stakes. "Answer or else extreme measures will be taken," one of them bellows.

My mind races with terrifying possibilities of what they'll do to me—and I know there is nothing I can do to stop it. With a trembling voice, I answer their questions, trying desperately to stay alive.

The torture starts. One of them retrieves a knife from the corner of the room and slices deep into my skin as he repeats the same questions again and again. The pain is unbearable, but I grit my teeth and bite back my cries of agony. It feels like an eternity before they finally stop. Prayers slip past my lips, but they go unanswered—instead, Isaac's henchmen enter and stand over me, their faces twisted in amusement.

"It was all a misunderstanding," they say mockingly. "You should have thought twice about getting yourself caught in a room with another man's naked wife alone."

It wasn't like that, I want to say. But I know it will only make it worse. I also know they are messing with me, playing mind games, trying to break me down. "Get up, let's go."

I shake my head hard, even though I know it won't make any difference. Fear snakes up inside me, cold and heavy and thick, gripping my throat so tight that I can't even speak—I just pray for a miracle that will never come. As realization hits home—I'll never see my daughter again—the boys laugh cruelly, reveling in their control.

They untie me and pull me to stand on my trembling legs. As they drag me out of the room, all I can feel is the ice-cold touch of a gun barrel against my temple.

30

Abby

I fiddle with the key card for a moment before pushing open the door to our cabin, my heart heavy and hope waning. But my steps falter when I hear my name called from inside.

Dad is standing there, looking like a ghost. I can't believe my eyes. I can't believe he's here. I didn't know if I'd ever see him again. A huge lump pushes up in my throat, and I swallow hard against the pressure. I've never been happier.

When our eyes meet, a current of elation and relief passes through me that nearly knocks me off my feet. His blue eyes glint against the darkening bruises around them, and there are raw wounds on his arms and face.

He stumbles toward me with outstretched arms and pulls me in for a crushing embrace. I can't fight back the tears as I bury my face deep in his chest, feeling each heavy breath tremble through him like thunder.

Finally he frees himself from my grip, holding me at arm's

length so he can get a look at me. "Are you okay?" he whispers tenderly.

"Am I okay? Yes, Dad," I whisper back, fighting for every word. "But are you?"

A small, exhausted smile twitches across his face as he struggles to stand. He's dressed in rags, with dark bruises peppering his arms and shoulders. Even from a distance I see small cuts dance along his cheekbones, and the stark contrast of his black eye against his pale skin.

He reaches up to touch it before I can intervene. "It looks worse than it is."

"It looks pretty bad," I say. "Come sit down."

I help him over to the couch, not realizing how badly he's limping until we get there. Then I see the smears of blood on his pants. "Oh God..." What happened to him?

"It's just a few flesh wounds," he lies. But I don't believe him for a second. "Nothing major."

"Can I get you something? Should I call a doctor?"

Fear flickers in his eyes as he says, "I don't know...let me think. I'm not sure I want to draw attention to myself—or make matters worse by being exposed to someone who has been around people with the virus."

"I think you need a doctor," I tell him firmly.

"For now, just some water, okay?"

My heart aches as I fill up a glass for him. He rolls up his pant leg then winces when he sees the full extent of the damage done to his leg. What if those cuts get infected?

Dad notices my worry and offers an explanation. "I'm going to use the antibiotics Dr. Clifford prescribed you. Can you grab them?"

"Sure," I reply quickly before adding, "Are you hungry? I have a sandwich..."

He laughs dryly— his usual joking manner returning despite

the pain and exhaustion evident on every inch of him. "I'm starving! I could eat an elephant!"

We huddle together on the sofa, wolfing down Molly's sandwich. But soon his smile fades and the weight of his experience drags him into darkness. His hands shake, and tears stream down his cheeks. I tighten my grip around him, aching at the thought of how he's suffering.

He leans against me with a sigh, resting his head on my shoulder as if shedding all of his anxieties that were locked away. His body trembles as gut-wrenching sobs rack through him, letting go all of what had happened. We stay like that for an eternity, until his breathing evens out and exhaustion takes over.

He pulls back, wiping away the last of his tears. "I'm sorry," he whispers before leaning against me once again. I've never been so relieved to see him and vow never to give him grief again. "Do you want to talk now?"

"No," he says with a heavy voice. "I want to sleep."

"Can I get you anything else? Ice?"

"My first aid kit is in my bag—would you be able to grab it?"

I'm rummaging through his luggage when he speaks up. "Blake was just here asking for you—he looked surprised to see me..."

"Did he say anything?" I ask, hoping the answer is no. I really don't want Roger to know about my search for Morgan. I'll tell him soon, but now is not the time. Not only because of his condition or the fact he'll feel betrayed, but because it will open up a whole can of worms I'm not ready for. If he finds out she is on this boat, and that is the reason I coaxed him into this trip, chances are he may never speak to me again. "Dad?"

"Huh?"

"I asked if Blake said anything."

Roger shakes his head. "No, just that he was checking in on you."

"He's been a lifesaver," I say.

"That's good," Dad says, closing his eyes. "But I'm here now."

31

Roger

The sun was beginning to break through the dense fog that had enveloped us for what seemed like an eternity. Abby and I stepped onto the deck of the ship, feeling a wave of relief wash over us as the salty spray of the sea hit our skin. Despite the oppressive heat of the cabins, the air was surprisingly cool outside, which was a welcome change.

The crew had been rationing the AC for days now, citing concerns over fuel, though I wasn't sure I believed them. Isaac and his crew had a penchant for making others suffer, and I had my suspicions that there was something else going on.

Suddenly, Blake jogs up to us. "Good to see you out and about. I came by twice, but there was no answer. It had me worried."

"I'm not big on visitors these days," I say. "Besides, where could we have gone?"

Abby smiles nervously. "Dad's not been feeling well."

The truth is worse—I can hardly breath, with my ribs still

broken and my body battered and bruised. Abby offered me some of her breathing treatments, but I can't bring myself to take medicine from my daughter. Who knows when or if we'll get more?

"Those are some nasty cuts," Blake remarks. "You sure you're okay to be out here? I could help Abby..."

"I'm fine," I say, thinking about how important it is not to let Isaac and his goons think they've won. "They're superficial. Nothing major."

This is a lie. I had to stitch myself up with a sewing kit I found in the room. But even though I am far from recovered, I cannot stay in that cabin for a second longer. I understand that if the enemy deems you useless, you are a dead man walking. Besides, I refuse to cower in fear. I refuse to send my daughter out alone.

We make our way to the pool deck, feeling the tension in the air; everyone seems to be looking over their shoulder at every turn.

Fear and anxiety have become a norm since the start of this trip. But today, it's different; there is a new edge in the air, a new frazzled energy. Abby and Blake exchange a glance, and I know they feel it too.

As we approach the pool, I see a familiar figure standing at the railing overlooking the ocean. It is Molly, and I'm not sure how to feel about seeing her. I suspect she has every bit to do with my release as she did my confinement, but I wouldn't know. There's been no contact ever since they let me go. She did, however, visit me once when I was in the brig. I'd been so delirious, so beaten down, that I thought I might have dreamed it. But when I woke up there was a sandwich tucked under the blanket in the corner, and I knew it was real. She had been there.

I picture her terrified face as she knelt at my side. "I'm going to get you out of here," she said. "I need you to hang on."

I don't know if I said anything back. But I do know that she had lifted my hand, turned my palm over and traced three letters into it. Slowly, so she could be sure I got it. *FBI.*

32

Abby

Molly spins around as we approach, startling me. "Good morning," she says. Her voice is calm and measured, but there is something off about her tone that I can't quite place.

I want to demand answers—did she deliberately set Dad up? Is she gunning for his demise? What is with the blatant public appearance?—but Molly has other plans.

"I have some bad news," she says gravely. "A new body has been found. A woman."

The words feel like a heavy mallet slamming into my stomach.

Roger warned me yesterday: If bodies keep dropping, they'll quarantine us here forever.

"The virus...?" Blake asks.

Molly immediately shakes her head, silencing him. "We don't believe it's related to the virus. There's a killer on board, and it isn't any of the Sons and Daughters folks."

Dad, Blake, and I all shoot one another concerned looks. "But how do you know?" I ask her.

"I can't say how. I just know."

Instinctively my gaze drifts toward the bridge. “We need to tell the captain.”

Molly shakes her head. "He already knows," she says. “He is taking measures to investigate, but he needs to do it discreetly. We can't afford to trigger any additional panic among the passengers.”

Darting my eyes to Roger, I stutter, "I bet it's those guys from the terminal—the ones that threatened us!"

He shakes his head slowly. "If it were them, they would have started by coming after me," he states quietly. "But I guess anything is possible."

Molly adds slowly, as if revealing secret information, "It was Chuck who had spoken to Isaac earlier this week. About you."

“What do we do now?” I ask.

Molly warns us to watch out for anything strange and stick together. We all shoot Blake a look as he coughs, fearing that he could be contagious.

"Everything on this ship is strange," he responds darkly.

“Anyway—I gotta go," Molly says. "I was hoping I'd run into you..."

As we make our way back to our cabin, I can feel the tension rising.

“We need to watch our backs,” Blake says. “We don’t know who we can trust. And I don't think Molly is someone I’d put my faith in, if I were you.”

“I don’t have much faith to put anywhere,” Dad says.

“I think this is one giant trap. Think about it—“ he continues. "She's with them. Of course, as we get closer to port, she's going to draw the attention off herself."

I agree with Blake.

But as the day wears on, I can’t shake the feeling we are being watched. Every time I turn a corner, I feel like someone is there, lurking in the shadows. The tension is almost unbearable.

As the night falls, I can't shake the feeling that something terrible is about to happen. We huddle together in our cabin, listening to the sounds of the ship, and each creak and groan of the deck feels like an omen of doom.

Suddenly, there is a loud banging on our door. I jump up, but Roger grabs my arm, pulling me back.

“Don’t open it,” he says.

But the banging continues, and I know we can't ignore it any longer. Dad approaches the door cautiously, waiting for a sign of who is outside.

"Isaac wants to see you," a rough voice says.

Roger and I exchange a look, and I know what this means. We have no choice but to go.

We hurry toward the bridge, Isaac and his gang already there. As we enter, I can see that something is different. The atmosphere is hostile and electric, and everyone is on edge.

Isaac breaks the uneasy silence. "It appears we have a rat in our midst," he hisses. "Someone who has been working against us from the start."

Roger stares at him, not daring to even breathe. I place a reassuring hand on his shoulder, fighting my own rising terror.

"We need your help to root out this traitor," Isaac says. "We know that you're not with us, but you can still help. You can be a part of our cause."

Dad snorts incredulously. I dig my elbow into his side, remembering too late that it's still bruised from their attack. “Your cause?” he gasps. “You almost killed me!"

“Sooner or later, we all die,” Isaac emphasizes darkly.

The desperation in his voice sends icy fingernails down my spine. Everyone exchanges nervous looks. Then Isaac's followers start to murmur among themselves, casting suspicious glances at us. I can feel their eyes on me, weighing me up, trying to determine whether I can be trusted.

"What do you want us to do?" I ask, trying to keep my voice from trembling.

Isaac fixes me with a smile that is more of a warning. "We need you to help us find the traitor," he says. "You'll be our eyes and ears on this ship."

I catch Dad's eye, and I know we feel the same way. We don't have a choice in this.

"Okay," I grit out, forcing confidence into my voice. "What do we have to do?"

Isaac's grin broadens. "We have reason to believe that the traitor might be someone you know," he says. "We need you to keep an eye on everyone, observe their movements, and report back to us."

I nod, trying to mask my emotions. I'm aware of the danger, but there's no other way around it.

"Good," Isaac says. "Begin with Molly."

I feel a jolt of surprise at his words, and I can tell from Dad's expression that he feels the same way.

"You like my wife, yeah?" Isaac says. "You wanted to take her from me, didn't you?"

Roger doesn't argue, even though I want him to. He simply says, "You have seven more."

"Not funny," Isaac snaps and motions for one of his men to take action.

The guy punches Roger in the gut, causing Dad to fall backward onto the floor. I rush toward him, attempting to break his fall, yet it's no use.

"Now show them back to their cabin," Isaac orders while keeping his eyes on Dad.

Once we're out of earshot, I whirl on Dad. "What are you doing?"

"Relax," he says calmly. "When your adversary is revealing themselves, do not stop them, but take good notes."

33

Abby

I wasn't expecting to run into Blake as I'm collecting our water rations, but I'm glad I do. Roger is burning up with fever, and I need to find my mother sooner rather than later. I'm terrified of something happening to him. Dad needs medical attention, but no one will listen, least of all him.

"Find anything?" I ask, tapping Blake's shoulder.

He glances away, looking almost annoyed at being bothered.

"I'm sorry to keep asking," I say quickly, feeling embarrassed. "It's just I haven't told Roger—my dad—and if he found out I'm trying to locate Mom he wouldn't understand."

Blake's expression softens sympathetically. "I understand. Actually, I was hoping you'd come by," he says.

He glances at me guiltily and quickly adds, "Without your dad knowing, of course. I don't want to cause any trouble—I consider Roger a friend."

A laugh sputters out of me. "That's smart," I say, "because Roger doesn't have many friends left to lose."

His brow furrows in thought for a moment before he brightens and says, "Anyway—yes, I have found something…"

My heart races with anticipation as he continues. "I've finished my search of the ship's records," he says. "I'm sorry, but there's no sign of your mother on board."

The hope that had been blossoming inside me shrivels away, and my stomach drops in disappointment. I had been hoping against hope that Morgan might have stowed away on board the ship, but Blake's words dash that possibility.

"Do you think she could have gotten off the ship before it left port?" I ask. "I was sure she'd be on board..."

He shakes his head. "I'm sorry, but that doesn't seem likely."

His expression shifts and he adds, "I do have one question for you though—did you know she was a member of that cult?"

I don't know what to say. I suppose I knew he'd figure it out. I just wasn't prepared for what would happen when he did. I hope this doesn't mean he'll stop helping me now. He is quite fond of Roger. I have no doubt he'll mention it to him when he gets the chance.

"What?" I gasp. "No, I didn't know."

Molly strides onto the deck and pins Blake, then me, with her intense gaze. "We need to talk," she says in a voice as sharp as her eyes, and my heart leaps into my throat. Did she find out about our deal with Isaac?

"What is it?" I ask, steeling myself for what she might say next.

Molly purses her lips and looks away without answering me, and dread pools in my gut.

I turn to Blake and force out a smile, but inside, I'm panicking. "I have to go."

"Of course," he says. "Just let me know if you need anything else."

I manage a genuine, gratitude-filled smile this time, but just before I can walk away, something stops me. I spin around to face him again. "Do you think my mother is still alive?"

He draws in a long breath before answering. “I have no reason to think she wouldn’t be.”

“It's just—I feel like there’s something you’re not telling me.”

He gives the faintest of nods without breaking our stare. “I don't want to cross your father…but I looked at the company HR records,” he reveals quietly. “According to tax statements, your Mom is living in the Virgin Islands and working at a resort there.”

My suspicions were right. He was hiding something from me.

“If you come by my cabin later,” he continues, “I can get you the address.”

34

Passenger 327

There comes a moment in every game of poker where the bluff is over. I stand over Jenna, my feet firmly planted on the hardwood floor. She's bound tight to the bed, her wrists chafing against the rope with every movement. Sweat slips down her forehead and cheeks as she whimpers about the heat radiating from the walls, smothering her like a blanket.

"One more sound," I growl, "and it'll be me smothering you instead."

She rolls her eyes like it's a dare.

I step closer and attempt to lock eyes with the defiant young woman before me.

"We don't have much time left," I say, pacing back and forth in front of her. "You've been here days now and still no progress."

She remains silent, her jaw tense like a taunt, inviting me to keep talking.

"Look," I say, "you need to become Anna if you want to be free.

And that won't happen if you keep this up. You need to learn how to be docile and compliant, or I can't help you."

"I'm not Anna!" she snaps. "I don't even know who she is."

I stop my pacing and stare at Jenna, my voice icy calm. "You need to become her," I say. "Act as she would, think as she would—or else I'm afraid I'll have to kill you…"

She nods hesitantly, her lips trembling with fear. Though I have no reason to feel guilt or remorse for what I am about to do, I can't shake the feeling that something inside me was dying along with her.

"There's only one problem," Jenna stammers, her body shaking with fear. "If I don't know who she is, how can I be her?"

My heart sinks deep into my stomach; a chasm of regret and sorrow threatens to swallow me alive. To help ease her conscience, I move closer and gently place my hand on her cheek.

I smile—a desperate person is an exploitable person. "The truth is," I whisper, "you're right. That's why I'm here—to help you find out. Let's make love again—that ought to help..."

Jenna looks away, her eyes stinging with unshed tears. She's not ready to accept my offer yet, but I must be patient. This has to be her choice, even when it comes to making love.

Softening my voice, I say, "I know this must be difficult for you, but think about it: If you become Anna, you will be happier. You won't have to worry about Bo or Heather anymore—or their pesky parents coming after you. You'll be free."

Jenna closes her eyes and takes a deep breath. I could see her trembling as she battles with my suggestion.

"I don't think you're ready to die," I venture.

"All right," she says finally. "Let's try."

I nod and go to the nightstand, retrieving a small box full of jewelry—earrings, a necklace, a bracelet, and a ring.

"These are for you," I explain. "They will help you become Anna."

Jenna examines each piece of jewelry, methodically feeling the weight of them in her hands as she touches them.

"She was wearing them when she died," I utter solemnly.

She nods almost imperceptibly, as if she'd known it all along. “What do I do now?”

I grab the jewelry. "Let's put it on," I say. "Now, try to think of Anna. Imagine what she'd do, how she'd act, and what she'd say."

Jenna nods, and I help her take off her old trinkets. A wave of sadness washes over her as her identity slowly vanishes. She clasps on the new pieces and shuts her eyes, trying to channel the person she will become.

"One more thing," I say, scooting closer. I reach out and caress her face lightly. "Anna was beautiful, Jenna. You are too. Can you feel her in you?"

Jenna's eyes flutter as if in a trance before regaining focus.

"Yes," she chokes out, trembling. "I wanna be Anna. I want to be free."

My breath tickles her ear as I murmur, "That's good, sweetheart, but you know, Anna had very particular tastes... particular desires..."

"I know what she wants," Jenna answers, her voice full of lust. She shivers in anticipation, her eyes locked on mine. "I can feel what she wants."

Tossing away all my inhibitions—the ones that made me feel remorse, pity, fear—I continue, “How do you know?”

“I've always known,” Jenna replies in a trembling voice.

My breath is hot against her neck as I push further. She has gotten so good at this game. "Tell me then, Jenna—what does Anna want?"

She breathes out a single word—an invitation — as she whispers back: "She wants you to take her... to make her yours."

I press my lips to her ear, my words as soft as a whisper. "Take control, Anna. You're in charge now. Feel how wet you get..."

Jenna takes in a deep breath, and a tiny moan escapes her lips.

"Show me," I say. "Let me see how you get off."

My body moves closer to hers, my hand tracing the curves of her body until it reaches between her legs. Her mouth pops open slightly, eyes glazing over with desire.

"Please," she begs.

"Please what?" I ask, barely above a whisper.

"Touch me...please touch me there."

My fingers do as they're told, and she gasps, the sound filling the room.

"Do you feel that?" I ask breathlessly.

"Yes," she whispers back, her voice trembling with anticipation.

A little louder this time, I say, "If you're going to be Anna, you have to get wet faster..."

I push down on her stomach, forcing myself deeper inside her. She moans again, a little louder this time. But I know she's faking.

"You like that?" I ask.

"Yes," she pants.

"You want more?"

"Yes."

"Liar!" I say. "You're a fucking liar."

I wrap my hands around her throat, and I'm about the finish her off, when there's a knock at the door.

35

Roger

I strain my ears, listening for the sound of Abby's footsteps on the deck as she disappears around the corner. I noticed her slipping out of the cabin, so I followed her. I'm hoping to find out what she is up to. Something's off, and although I'm uncertain of her destination, my gut tells me where she's headed.

She thinks I'm ill, and while I'm not entirely in perfect health, I might have exaggerated a bit. How else could I draw the fox out of its hole?

I keep a safe distance, not wanting her to realize I'm tailing her. I figure perhaps she is sneaking out to meet that boy again, but when she appears at Blake's door, my suspicions immediately shift. I know this is something more sinister than teenage rebellion. Blake isn't someone Abby should be spending time with, and the thought of him preying on my daughter fills me with a rage I haven't felt before.

I'm not about to let a grown man take advantage of my daughter.

Panic slams into me as I realize what he could do to Abby if I don't act fast.

Blake opens the door and lets Abby inside, despite the late hour, and I can tell there is something the two of them are hiding, something I don't know about. Fury surges through me, and I know I have to intervene.

Molly's universal keycard is still in my pocket—the one that can open any door on the ship. The thought of what it might unlock flashes through my mind, and I snatch it out. I charge toward the cabin and let myself in.

My pulse is pounding as I burst into the room—and then I see him: Blake towering over Abby with his hands around her neck. Red-hot fury floods my veins. Without hesitation, I launch myself at him. First, I grab hold of his arms. Then I yank him off my daughter with a violent force. After that, I pummel his head and torso with my fists, elbows, whatever. I stomp his face into the carpet—I let into him with everything I've got.

A voice cuts through my rage. A faint but trembling cry. "Stop, Dad," Abby pleads, tears streaming down her face.

The knot inside me goes slack with relief that my daughter is unharmed. I snatch her hand and hustle us out of the room. Just before we reach the door, a woman's cries echo from the closet. It sends icy undercurrents through my veins.

I stop dead in my tracks, my grip still tight around Abby's hand. The woman's voice is muffled, but I can hear her gasping for air. I know what's happened. My stomach churns with revulsion.

I glance at Abby, who is staring at me with a mix of fear and confusion.

She shakes her head. She refuses to go, but I nudge her toward the door. I can't let her stay and bear witness to horrors no child should ever endure. It breaks my heart to see her fear, but she's in shock. She's too stunned to move.

"Go," I say, pushing her toward the door.

She shakes her head again. "I can't."

The woman in the closet continues to sob and plead for help as I make my way back across the room toward Blake. He's slumped on the floor, beaten unconscious, but this isn't justice—men like Blake need to understand vengeance in its purest form.

I approach him as if he were a wild animal ready to pounce on his next victim. The sight of him brings my rage boiling to the surface. Without hesitation, I grab the lamp from the nightstand and swing it at his slumped figure. I strike him in the head again and again, uncontrollable rage surging through me, until he no longer moves.

My heart hammers in my chest as I realize that the threat has been neutralized. A flood of relief washes over me like a wave, followed by revulsion when I take stock of what has occurred in this room. Everywhere I look, I see overturned furniture, shattered glass and spilled blood—everything that could have happened to my daughter if I hadn't been able to enter.

I tense up, fear crawling up my spine like smoke. Guilt creeps in as I feel like I failed my daughter. But then I remember the woman in the closet, and all thoughts of self-pity vanish.

I take a deep breath and approach the closet with caution, not knowing what to expect. Inside there is a young woman in her early twenties, gagged and bound with duct tape. She looks at me with desperation in her eyes and I act fast, ripping the tape off her mouth so she can take a much needed breath of air. Tears stream down her face as she stares at me pleadingly.

"Please help me," she whispers hoarsely.

"What's your name?"

She looks away, like she can't—or won't answer.

"I'm Roger."

"Jenna," she says as she weeps. "My name is Jenna."

36

Abby

The oppressive air seems to weigh us down, an invisible blanket of fear and despair. Roger insists I'm in shock, but my senses are razor sharp: The waves lapping against the boat reverberate in my ears, and Blake's blood lingers on my father's hands despite his scrubbing.

Tension hangs between Jenna, huddled on the couch with her arms wrapped around her knees, and me and Roger facing each other across the cabin.

My father strips off his bloodied shirt, revealing a chest marred with mottled bruises. Worry creases his forehead as he stares at me for what feels like eons before saying, “Just let me think for a minute, okay?”

"I don't want to go to the cops," Jenna whispers. "We don't have to tell anyone…”

She begs us with wide, frightened eyes.

"Of course we do," Roger and I answer in unison.

Her plea reverberates between us, seeping into our bones. We both know we can't keep this a secret. It would be foolish to think that we would get away with it. I know my dad well enough to understand that he'd never shirk away from doing the right thing.

Roger draws a long breath before responding. "Jenna, what happened is serious. You can't just sweep it under the rug and hope it goes away."

She looks at him with pleading eyes, her lower lip trembling. "But if anyone finds out—if anyone finds out about…" She trails off, unable to finish the sentence.

Dad's mouth forms a thin line straight line. "We have to do the right thing. Maybe not now, but eventually this *will* come out."

I want to reach out and tell her it's all going to be okay, but I can't find the words. My mind is still spinning.

Roger's mood shifts. His face is contorted with rage, and I know he's thinking of what just happened in Blake's cabin.

I shiver as I remember what he did, and what my father did in return. I tried to look away from the violence before me, but I could not. I was rooted in place, my eyes locked on my father, my heart beating a frantic rhythm in my chest.

I'd never seen that side of him.

Jenna's mood shifts in proportion to Dad's. She has tears streaming down her cheeks, desperation written across her face.

"Please," she begs. "I'll go back to my room and pretend none of this ever happened. I saw nothing, and neither did you."

Jenna insists we shouldn't draw attention to ourselves. She says we can't risk calling security. She just wants off the ship, she wants to disappear, and this is the only way.

"They'll have to come eventually," I say. "The police; if there's been a murder."

"There have been lots of murders," Jenna replies quietly. "No one has come yet."

"They haven't been called," Roger grumbles. "Isaac won't allow it."

"He'll have to now," I reply. "Won't he?"

Dad shakes his head. "But eventually we'll dock, and the authorities will come. The truth will come out."

Jenna quickly interjects, "It doesn't have to... We can make it so nothing ever comes out."

Everyone goes silent for a moment, digesting the weight of Jenna's words.

Roger's face is etched with sadness and sympathy as he considers Jenna's plea. I can see the inner battle raging in him as he tries to decide what is best for us all to do. After thinking long and hard, his voice breaks the silence, low and resolute. "We have an obligation to report what happened."

He meticulously goes over the details of the event, speaking slowly and cautiously. "There's only one choice here," he states after a pause. "We must inform the authorities—or security for now—and disclose what we know. There's DNA evidence all over that room."

Jenna looks petrified, but she nods her head in agreement, tears streaming down her cheeks without cease. It's clear that this is our only way out if we wish to avoid jail time.

I clasp my hands together, trying hard not to cry too. We are in way over our heads, and I'm afraid of what will happen next. Who is actually in charge of this ship? The Sons and Daughters of Infinity? The captain they installed? If they find out Dad killed Blake, what will they do? He's already been under enough scrutiny as it is. Maybe Jenna has a point. Maybe we say nothing until we dock.

Roger reaches for the telephone, yet hangs it up seconds later with a heavy sigh. "It doesn't work."

I sit there motionless, my mind spinning as I attempt to process everything.

"It's best if we gather our rations," he suggests solemnly. "Who knows if I'll be thrown in the brig again, and I can't let you go hungry."

"Why the brig?" I exclaim. "It was self-defense!"

“Not exactly.” His lips tighten into a frown. “And we're not exactly dealing with a sane bunch.”

My gaze flits to Dad. "Maybe Jenna is right. We should wait."

He speaks in a comforting tone. "She's been through a lot, honey. She needs help, too."

"You don't understand," Jenna interjects. “I’ve killed people before.”

37

Roger

The only thing that never changes is... everything always and constantly changes. The world is spinning out of control around me; the deafening shrieks of terror and desperation silence any chance of logic in my mind.

My suggestion that we collect our rations was two-fold: We've been without water for nearly a day, and I need to find Molly. If anyone will know what to do—or how to get through to Isaac to allow us to dispatch the Coast Guard—it will be her.

A haze of panicked murmurs and hissing whispers smothers the air like a thick blanket, making it hard to focus. Wind slashes against my skin like an icy blade. A storm is coming, and everyone can feel it.

I glance out at the tumultuous sea before resuming my search. I keep an eye out for Molly while shouting Abby's name. The atmosphere is thick with panic and despair. I watch as people flee, others cower and hide, and a few stand still, paralyzed in anticipation of what's to come.

My heart slams against my ribcage as I hunt for Abby in the tumultuous crowd. Hundreds of faces swell around me, but nothing can prepare me for the terror that consumes me when she's not in my sight.

"Abby!" I shout, the sound swallowed up by the roiling ocean. Relief washes over me as I spot her on the other side of the deck. She's standing in the breadline. She looks shell-shocked, eyes wide with fatigue from a long, insufferable night without water—the same look I wear draped across my features. I still cannot comprehend the recklessness of my decision to board this vessel—how foolish I was to take such a risk. Pushing through the mass of people, the horror surrounding us slams into me like a brick wall. But Abby is all I can focus on—getting her safely back to land.

I watch her move toward the rations line. Even from here, I can make out the exhaustion carving into her face and posture. She has aged beyond what she should be at just sixteen—illness, and now this trip, have seen to that. Nothing can prepare you for this kind of devastation. My little girl, stripped of her innocence and forced to bear witness to a world filled with last resorts and limited hope.

She grabs two loaves of bread with a triumphant grin. I feel relieved. We now have water and food. We are okay at the moment.

The sudden silence that falls onto the deck forces my heart rate to skyrocket—and then I see it reflected in Abby's expression: terror.

A man steps forward, gun in hand and aimed at us all.

My heart lurches into my throat. I have to get to Abby before he pulls the trigger. But I know it will be too risky. Suddenly, bullets are being sprayed everywhere, and there is no guarantee I will make it across safely.

I know my best bet is to go around, but that will take time—time I don't have. The alternative is to run straight into gunfire, an untenable plan in any situation.

By the time I reach the other side of the deck, the sirens are wailing, and desperate voices fill the air. With every step I take, I can feel the weight of the horror pressing down on me, and everywhere I look is carnage—broken bodies strewn across the deck in rivers of red blood.

I sprint in search of my daughter among the chaos, dodging bullets and shattered glass. On some level, I am aware of something else, too—the cries of people who have lost loved ones and their own frightened screams for help and safety.

"ABBY!" I bellow, my voice reverberating through the masses as I push forward, desperate to reach her. It feels like an eternity since I last laid eyes on my daughter. I am terrified of what I'll find.

My eyes dart around the deck, trying to find her. And then I spot her—lying there, clutching loaves of bread with a white-knuckle grip. Through teary eyes, Abby throws an obscenity up to the heavens. Is she flipping off the gunman? Me? God? I can't tell.

I scoop her up in my arms. My relief is short-lived when I notice the bright red splattered across her shirt—like an omen of what is to come. Gently, I peel away the fabric, only to find a gaping wound festering beneath. The sight makes my stomach drop and a cold sweat wash over me.

She stares up at me, her pale face twisted with fear as she whispers, "My stomach—"

I take a deep breath and cup her head in my hands. Our gazes lock as I say, "It's not that bad. You're gonna make it through this."

And with that one sentence, she seems to believe me.

38

Roger

I lurch forward and clutch Abby's hands, but they slip away in a pool of crimson. I frantically press my hands down on her stomach, trying to stave off the relentless flow of blood, but it is too late. I can feel her life force fading from her body.

Desperate, I scan the deck for help—but all I see is chaos and panic as people scramble away from the scene. I know I must act fast, yet I am blocked by Isaac's security team. No one will move out of the way because, in their mind, saving Abby is not important enough compared to saving themselves.

"There are too many wounded," one guard calls out over the roar of the crowd. "Why should she take priority? The Sons and Daughters of Infinity come first."

"She's just a child," I plead through tears. "She's only sixteen—"

"Let her die," another guard responds coldly. "She isn't one of us."

Time is running out, and my heart sinks as I look into Abby's pale face—fearing she will succumb to her gunshot wound before help arrives. I beg the guards to allow me to get her help, but they remain steadfast in their stance.

Then, a booming voice echoes throughout the deck. It is Isaac leading his followers in prayer.

The murmuring crowd grows silent until only Isaac's commanding words can be heard ringing across the loudspeakers.

"The end days are upon us," he proclaims with conviction. "We must all accept our fates and prepare for the coming storm."

As I look into Abby's pale face, I know that we're all in grave danger if this man continues to hold sway over these people onboard.

The cult's chants fill the air and the security team steps back. I have only a moment to act. I scoop Abby up in my arms and bolt away, sprinting through the ship. Everywhere is chaos and despair.

I feel like time has frozen when I reach the medical bay and burst in, screaming for help, but they won't let me pass. I'm helpless, silently begging for a miracle as my throat tightens.

Just as I'm about to give up hope, two young men rush out from the back of the med bay. "Give her to me," one says. "I'll get her help."

He looks familiar—it's that kid from the nightclub. His pants are smeared with a dark red, and his hands have small specks of blood on them. "Where?"

"We've got a room set up down the hall," he continues, pointing ahead. But before I can move an inch, he clamps a hand on my shoulder and shakes his head. "You'll have to wait here."

My heart races in my chest while panic rises in my throat. "I'm not going to let you take my daughter."

"You don't have another choice," he says. "If you want her to live, I need to take her now."

"We have a doctor. He can help her."

The other boy steps forward, placing his hand on my shoulder.

His eyes are brown and warm and slanted like a cat's. He introduces himself as Luke.

"Believe me," he says. "We'll do everything we can to save her."

A wave of conflicting emotions wash over me—fear of leaving her in the hands of a stranger coupled with desperation to do anything to save her life. I know I have no other options left. I reluctantly hand Abby over to Luke, praying that he is telling the truth and she will receive the help she needs.

As they disappear into the back of the medical bay, I fall to my knees, overwhelmed with grief and despair. I can't bear the thought of losing Abby, the only person in my life who truly matters.

Hours pass, and I am still waiting in the medical bay, pacing anxiously back and forth. There are other wounded passengers receiving treatment, but I can't bring myself to care. All I can think about is Abby and whether she is still alive.

39

Roger

I shiver in the medical bay, the antiseptic smell clinging to the air. I'm immobile, slumped in a rigid plastic chair, my body weighed down with dread and my head spinning with unanswerable questions. I think of Jenna, back in our cabin, probably wondering where we are, if we're ever coming back. Wondering if we're among the dead. Maybe she even hopes we are and that our little secret—Blake—died with us.

Molly rushes in, looking distraught. "Roger—how's Abby?"

The words escape me before I can stop them. "I don't know."

She moves closer to me, placing a comforting hand on my shoulder as she speaks. "It's going to be all right," she says. "Abby will pull through—I promise. She's a strong girl."

But the reassurance falls flat on my ears—it's impossible to believe. How did this happen? How could my daughter be fighting for her life? It all seems unreal.

Footsteps echo down the corridor, and we both look up as a

doctor appears in the doorway. He looks worn out as he addresses me.

"Mr. Atkins," he begins, his voice grave. "I'm afraid I have some bad news. The bullet punctured her intestines, and we're doing our best to repair the damage—to save her. But as this is not a proper hospital, there is only so much we can do."

He pauses for a moment before adding, "We cannot predict what the outcome will be yet."

My heart sinks as I hear his words. I have so many questions, but I just can't bring myself to ask any of them—all I do is bow my head and try to keep myself together, grief squeezing around my chest like an iron fist.

Molly reaches out and puts her arm around me, as if to try to take away some of my pain. But it is no use.

The doctor continues. "We have done all we can for now," he says. "But I'm afraid your daughter is in very critical condition. We will keep you informed of any changes, but right now, there's nothing more we can do except wait."

"Thank you," I say, trying to contain the desperation and fear clawing at me from within.

Molly nods. "Thank you, Jim."

"A friend of yours?"

"He's a Son of Infinity, yes."

I pause, my mind spinning with confusion. "I need you to persuade your husband to call for help. There are so many wounded—or dead—we can't just stand by and let them die. Abby included."

Molly shakes her head. "I've tried. He has other plans..."

My rage bubbles to the surface. "I—"

"He's going to sink the ship, Roger."

"With your credentials, you can't get word out?"

Her face is grim as she admits the truth. "I didn't get on this ship expecting this would happen."

"None of us did."

An eerie silence fills the room, broken only by our shallow breaths. I finally break it.

“Molly,” I say firmly. “I need to find that gunman and then your husband.”

She shakes her head again, her complexion ashen. “I don't think that's a good idea.”

"I don't care," I grit out between clenched teeth.

"The gunman is dead," she reveals quietly.

My anger boils over into words. "Was he one of you? Is this your people's idea of a mass suicide?"

“He wasn't one of us. Just a crazed and panicked crew member. They’ve been under an extraordinary amount of pressure…”

“Jesus, Molly. Look around,” I say, gesturing wildly. “We’re all under an immense amount of pressure. But don’t go excusing the behavior of a mass murderer—it makes you sound evil.”

“I’m not excusing anything. I’m studying to be a profiler, Roger. It’s what I do.”

I look at Molly and realize that she is just as scared and confused as I am. “Sure, whatever.”

She fiddles nervously with her wedding ring. “Roger, there's something I need to tell you.” It feels like the air has been sucked out of my lungs. "What?" I croak, barely able to form the word. “What now?”

She takes a deep, shuddering breath and looks away from me. “Abby had been communicating with the cult,” she says, her voice shaking. “She *wanted* to join them on their ‘end of days’ journey.”

I feel the truth of her words like a weight in my chest, a truth I hadn’t wanted to hear.

"You're serious?"

“Sadly, yes.”

A leaden feeling settles in my stomach as I think back to all the times Abby had mentioned this trip. I had assumed she'd been interested in the all you can eat buffet, or sunbathing by the pool, not joining up with some fanatics who believe the world is ending.

My mind is spinning, yet I remain silent, unable to wrap my head around the betrayal I am feeling.

"That's not all," Molly says. "I don't think they have any intention of giving her back."

"What?" My head snaps in her direction. "They can't just keep her. She wouldn't allow it—I won't allow it."

"You have no idea what these people are capable of, Roger."

"And what about you?" I say. "Why aren't *you* doing more to help? Why haven't you *called* out for help?"

"They won't let me near the bridge," she replies. "How can I?"

"So all this sneaking around, and your hands are tied?" I shake my head. "I'm not buying it."

She sighs and looks down at her hands. "I know it's hard to understand, but I have my own reasons for being here. Reasons that I can't explain to you right now." She looks up at me. "I don't want to die, Roger. These people will kill me without a second thought. You understand that, don't you?"

"I've experienced what they can do—you saw me in the brig, remember?"

"It's getting to the point where I'm going to have to make a choice."

"A choice?" I shake my head, feeling like I'm at my wit's end. "What the hell is going on here, Molly?"

She looks up at me, her eyes filled with sadness. "We're not going to make it out of this alive, Roger. None of us are."

A shiver slithers up my spine. "What are you talking about?"

"The Sons and Daughters of Infinity, they believe in the end of the world, you know that. You've heard them espousing their nonsense—"

"Yeah, so?"

"So, they believe they are the only ones who will be saved. And they will do whatever it takes to make sure that happens. When I said they were going to try to sink the ship, I meant it."

My mind races as I digest her words. I look down at my bloodied shoes and then up at her. "What in the hell are we going to do?"

40

Roger

I survey the anxious faces before me, dim light casting sinister shadows on their features. This meeting was Molly's idea, her response to my question: *What in the hell are we going to do?*

My heart thumps heavily as I tell them about Abby's abduction by Isaac's cult, their refusal to tell me where on the ship she is, or if she's even still alive. Sweat beads down my back, but I power through the fear, steeling myself to motivate the fourteen people who agreed to show up.

Fourteen out of the eighty something that we asked. Jenna, Molly, and I, we went cabin to cabin personally, inviting people we thought we might be able to trust. People that might be useful. Most of the passengers on board are incredibly wealthy—they have no inclination to lift a finger, no survival skills. They are certain rescue is imminent.

"Isaac and his followers took my daughter Abby from me," I

say, my voice cracking. "No one else should have to go through this kind of hell."

Molly strides forward, her eyes blazing with determination. She passes out cult T-shirts and asks everyone to put them on. This way, they'll be able to move about the ship more freely, at least until they catch on. She explains that she has been working behind the scenes to bring Isaac and his deranged cult down.

"Roger is right. We have to stand together against the Sons and Daughters of Infinity. They've caused enough pain. They plan to sink the ship as a part of their quest for salvation—and we believe they'll follow through with their plan."

The passengers shift uncomfortably, their eyes darting between Molly and me. I can feel their disbelief, their uncertainty, their reluctance to get involved in something so dangerous. Then, a slender figure emerges from the group.

"They've taken my brother," Maria declares in an unwavering tone, despite her tears. "I don't know where—but I won't rest until justice is served."

Hope shoots through me as the words settle on us all. The first step of a unified front against Isaac and his gang has been taken, though dread lingers in the air like thick smoke.

"Maria's right," I say, my heart practically thumping out my chest. "We need to stand together if we have any hope of seeing our loved ones again." The words echo through the room, heavy with the weight of responsibility.

"There's strength in numbers," Maria adds, her eyes scanning the anxious faces before us. "We can't let them tear us apart. If we don't do something, we will *all* die…"

At first, their gazes remain downcast, the fear and uncertainty still palpable. But then, a middle-aged man raises his head to meet my stare.

"Isaac has brainwashed my daughter," he murmurs, the raw pain in his voice making my stomach twist. "I don't know what to do, but we can't just stand idly by while they destroy our lives."

As he speaks, others begin to share their own stories, hesitance giving way to anger and determination. From young couples thinking of their children back home, to the grieving family members of those killed by the gunman, each tale of loss and despair fuels our desire for action.

"Okay," says an elderly woman, her voice barely audible but brimming with resolve. "If we're going to do this, we have to stick together. We have to be a united front."

"Damn right," another passenger chimes in, his knuckles white as he clenches his fists. "Let's put an end to that bastard and his sick cult."

The room buzzes with a newfound sense of camaraderie, the air crackling with shared purpose.

"Let's take back what's ours," I whisper, more to myself than anyone else. “Let’s get a call out for help—let’s get the hell off this ship. Together.”

And in that moment, even though the road ahead of us looks bleak, I know we can’t sit idly by and wait for the worst to happen. We must do something. We must fight back.

"All right," I say, raising my voice so everyone can hear me. "Our first priority is to arm ourselves and find food. We won’t get far if we're weak and hungry."

"Split up into small groups," Molly suggests, her eyes scanning the room as she takes charge. "Check everywhere—closets, storage rooms, any cabin you can gain access to. Anything we can use as a weapon or food source could be our ticket to survival."

"Let's stick to groups of three," I add, trying to project confidence despite the knot of anxiety in my gut. "It's safer that way."

The passengers nod grimly, their faces etched with determination. As we break off into groups, I feel a hand on my shoulder.

"Roger, I'm with you," says a man named Thomas. Tall and wiry, his beard streaked with gray, he has the air of someone who's been through hell and back. The kind of person you want by your side when shit hits the fan.

"Thanks, Thomas," I reply, clapping him on the back. "Let's get to work."

Together, we comb the ship, our eyes peeled for anything that might give us an advantage. The stark metal walls seem to close in around us, casting ominous shadows as we make our way deeper into the bowels of the vessel.

"Over here," Thomas calls out, his voice echoing through the dimly lit cargo hold. He's standing beside a stack of crates, prying open the lid with a crowbar.

"Find something?" I ask, straining to see what he's uncovered.

"About a dozen box cutters," he grunts, lifting one up for me to see. "Not much, but better than nothing."

"Better than nothing" doesn't exactly fill me with confidence, but I swallow my doubts and force a smile. "Good find, Thomas. Let's grab as many as we can and get them back to the others."

As we gather our meager arsenal, I can't help but wonder if it'll be enough. If these flimsy blades will be any match for the evil that awaits us. I keep a tight grip on the crowbar.

"Roger," Thomas says, his voice low and steady. "If you're gonna lead, you gotta lead."

"I *am* leading," I say, thinking of Abby.

He gives me the side eye. "Just keep your head on straight. Keep focused."

"I'm focused."

"I don't know, man. Sometimes it feels like you're a million miles away."

"I wish I were," I say, scanning the rest of the crates. "Say, we need to grab any knives we can from the kitchen—restaurants, wherever."

Thomas shakes his head. "I heard the cult confiscated 'em all a while back. Before rations even started."

"Doesn't hurt to look just in case they missed a few."

"Yeah. Hey, Roger?"

"Huh?"

Thomas turns to me with a hopeful glimmer in his eye. "I just wanted to say, in case you're all up in your head about it, we're gonna make it through this. We've got each other's backs, remember?"

I nod, trying to convince myself as much as him. "I know," I say, my grip tightening on the box cutter in my hand. "We're in this together."

41

Roger

"Roger, you need to see this!" Maria's voice breaks through the tension, her tone urgent but tinged with a note of hope. She and Jenna have returned from their search, their arms laden with cans and packages.

"Food," Jenna says, her relief palpable. "Enough to keep us going for a while."

"Good work," I say with a tight smile. But there's no time to celebrate; we have more pressing matters at hand.

"Thomas and I found some box cutters. It's not much, but it's something."

"Better than nothing," Maria agrees, her dark eyes filled with determination. "Show us how to use them."

"All right," Thomas says, stepping forward with unwavering confidence. "Gather 'round, everyone."

My cabin was small to begin with, but now that it's serving as storage for the supplies we've collected, plus more than a dozen people, it feels downright claustrophobic. We commandeered the cabin next door, opening the connecting doors, but we could use more space.

The passengers huddle together tightly, their expressions drawn and anxious, yet willing to learn. I observe as Thomas demonstrates the proper grip on the box cutter, his movements swift and precise despite the primitive weapon.

"Remember, the goal is separation between you and your attacker," he explains in a measured tone. "These blades aren't long, so you gotta be quick and deliberate with your strikes."

I chime in, showing the others how to lash out with the box cutter in rapid succession—slash after slash. A sharp fear still lingers, but there's something empowering about holding that blade—the knowledge that we won't go down without a fight.

"Stay alert," I caution them firmly, my voice tense. "Be ready for anything."

"Let's hope it doesn't come to that," Jenna mutters, her knuckles white as she grips her own box cutter.

"Agreed," I say, meeting her eyes. "But if it does, we'll be ready."

As we distribute the weapons and continue our impromptu training session, I can feel the tension in the room shift. We're still afraid—that much is clear—but beneath the fear, a quiet determination simmers. The kind that will steel our spines when we face Isaac's cult.

Maria and Jenna quickly portion the food into equal shares for each of us. It's a reminder that survival doesn't just rely on weaponry and strength; sustenance is needed, too—physical and mental nourishment.

"Here," Maria says, handing me a small cloth-wrapped bundle. "Make sure everyone gets one."

"Will do," I reply, feeling the package's weight in my hand. It won't last forever, but it'll have to do until we can get more provisions.

I pass out food rations among the passengers, listening to

snippets of their conversations: low tones laced with terror, rage, and sorrow. Yet beneath the hushed chatter lies something else—a spark of hope that refuses to be extinguished.

"Did you hear about what happened to Sarah?" someone whispers. “I heard they killed her—on deck, in front of everyone—just to set an example.”

"God, that's awful," another passenger murmurs. “But at least we're doing something about it.”

"Roger's right," a third voice chimes in, surprising me with its determination. “No way could we sit back and do nothing. We’d all be dead within the week.”

I nod, feeling the truth of their words even as my heart aches for the losses they've suffered. We've all lost something—or someone—to Isaac's twisted machinations. But now, in this moment, we have a chance to take back control, to fight for those we've lost and protect those who remain.

"All right, everyone," I announce, my voice carrying through the room. "Let's finish our preparations. We don't know when we'll need to act, so we need to be ready at a moment's notice."

The passengers exchange determined looks, clutching their box cutters and rations as they continue to train and prepare. Watching them, I can see the bonds forming between us—forged in blood and fear, but growing stronger with our newfound sense of purpose.

"Stay vigilant," I remind them again. “Don’t go out alone.”

When I look around at their determined faces, a knot of fear and doubt tightens in my gut. The responsibility of leading these people bears down on me like a crushing weight. I need a moment to breathe, to confide in someone who understands the darkness we're up against.

"Hey, Molly," I say, motioning her aside. "Could I talk to you for a moment?"

"Of course," she replies, concern etched on her face as she follows me to a quiet corner of the cabin.

"Listen, Molly," I begin, my voice barely above a whisper. "I'm scared." My hands tremble slightly, betraying my anxiety. "I've never been in a situation like this, and I feel like I'm in way over my head."

She looks at me with understanding, her eyes filled with empathy. "Roger, it's normal to be scared. This is an incredibly dangerous and unpredictable situation. But what matters is that you're stepping up, and you're doing everything you can."

Her words offer a slight comfort, but my doubts still claw at me. "But what if it's not enough? What if we fail, and more people get hurt because of me?"

She spins me around by the shoulders, forcing me to look into her eyes. "You can't think like that. It's normal to have doubts, but we have to trust in our abilities. We have to believe we're going to make it off this ship alive. Because if *you* don't believe this is true, no one else is going to."

I nod slowly, her conviction seeping into me. "You're right," I say. "Thank you. I... I guess I just needed to hear someone say it."

"Anytime," she says softly, giving my shoulder a reassuring squeeze. "But I agree with you on one thing..."

My brows raise. "What's that?"

"It's time for a concrete plan."

42

Roger

The sharp wind bites at my face as I lead Molly to a secluded spot on the ship's deck, away from the prying eyes and ears of other passengers. The darkness is only broken by the moonlight reflecting off the churning waves below us. We're on the deck where the shooting took place, and even though the crimson stains remain, in the dark you'd never know such an atrocity happened. It looks, mostly, like it did before.

"This is good," she says, stopping in her tracks. I can tell she doesn't want to go any further, and neither do I. It's eerie being here. "You think?"

"Should be," I reply, checking our surroundings for any eavesdroppers. "What's up?"

Molly bites her lip, her gaze furtively darting away from mine. I had assumed she'd asked me here to discuss the plan, but it's clear now that she's about to take a different direction. She takes a deep breath and speaks. “I thought we could catch up—as friends. I mean, I'd like to take the chance to get to know you better.”

“There’s not much to know.”

“Yeah?” she says. “Me either. To be honest, I have been a terrible workaholic. Back in Oregon, I always put my career first, working day and night, leaving no room for other things in life.” She looks away and then back at me. “Now, being here, I'm seeing the consequences of that approach.”

"Really?" I say with a sarcastic smirk. "A workaholic? I would have never guessed. You seem so…relaxed."

"Appearances can be deceiving, Roger," she says, not realizing I’m joking. I’d hoped to ease the tension, but it didn’t work.

Molly continues. “As an agent, I have been completely dedicated to my job. It's what led me to go undercover in the cult. I guess I could use some real friends—after *that. Nothing* is real with them, Roger. Nothing but the crazy, anyway.”

I stare at her, contemplating how to ease out of this conversation. They have my daughter, and I’m not in the mood for a romantic midnight stroll. Nor am sure I want to hear what I think she’s about to say. I just want to get on with it. "You don't have to justify yourself to me, Molly."

"I know that," she answers, gazing out at the dark horizon. “But I don't feel like anyone knows who I am, you know? And that's sad, considering the very real possibility that I could die here on this ship.”

"Okay," I say, realizing she wants me to take the bait. “Well then, who are you?”

She shrugs. "You know, I'm not sure even *I* know the answer to that anymore." She looks at me and then up at the sky. "For the past eight months, I've been Molly. But that's not really who I am."

"I thought you seemed a little too smart to agree to be some guy’s seventh wife."

"Eighth," she says with a wink.

I smile. “Wow. It’s even worse than I thought.”

"It sounds insane, I know. It wasn't easy, but it was necessary. I had to find out what they were planning, and the only way to do that was to become one of them."

The thought of Molly, of anyone, being part of that sick cult makes my stomach churn. I struggle to find the right words, but all I can think to say is, "Looks like it worked out well for you."

"Somewhat," she admits, her voice barely audible over the crashing waves. "But it's taken a toll on me."

"Understandably," I say. "I'm sure it's been difficult."

"Difficult doesn't even begin to cover it," she says, a pained smile on her face. "But it's worth it if no one else has to suffer."

She looks out at the water briefly before shifting her gaze back to mine. "Isaac has become a metaphor for evil, and there's a side of human nature that's fascinated by pure, unadulterated evil. Admittedly, I was, too—for a time. But the longer I've been around him, the more that narrative has diminished and given way to the truth: beneath all his theatrics, his bizarre ramblings, and his violent outbursts, Isaac's evil isn't magic, occult, or supernatural. He is just an average, everyday narcissist who understands social engineering and has learned to use the bodies of willing women around him as a bargaining tool."

The question slips out before I can stop it, my protective instincts kicking in. "He used *you* as a bargaining tool?"

"It was part of the job," she explains, her eyes pleading for understanding. "It wasn't real to me, but for him...he believed it. And that belief gave me access to information I needed. Isaac's supposed to be arrested when he steps off the boat."

My eyes widen. "No wonder he wants to sink the ship."

"Yeah, I have a feeling he knows. Or at least suspects. Men like him usually have a good sense of when the walls are closing in around them."

"God, Molly," I say, trying to wrap my head around the weight of her words. "This is bad. And by that, I mean, it keeps getting worse."

"Isaac is a master manipulator," she continues, her voice barely audible. "He controls everything—what people eat, when they sleep…even who they talk to."

Molly's eyes darken as she recounts her harrowing experiences within the cult, and I can't help but feel a deep empathy for her. The pain in her eyes speaks volumes about the strength it has taken her to endure so much in the name of a job. Even with my time in the military, I can't relate. It hardly feels like the same sacrifice.

"Roger, there's something else I need to tell you," she says, hesitating. Her voice is low and quiet, and I can see her struggling with whatever it is she wants to share.

"Oh God," I say, uneasiness surging through me.

She takes a deep breath and then looks me straight in the eye. "I've developed feelings for you, Roger. Your commitment to save your daughter...your kindness toward me...it's touched my heart."

My pulse races as Molly's confession hangs in the air between us. The dim lighting from a nearby window casts a soft glow on her face, highlighting her vulnerability. I'm stunned by her admission, unable to compute how to respond. My thoughts have been solely focused on Abby, not entertaining the possibility of a romantic connection.

My mind zips back to Morgan, Abby's mother, and all the unresolved feelings I still have for her.

"I, uh..." I stammer, surprised by this sudden shift in conversation. Finally, I find my footing. "Molly, I appreciate your honesty, but you need to understand...my daughter is everything to me at the moment. I can't get distracted."

"Please don't think I'm trying to get in the way of what we're trying to do here," Molly quickly adds, her cheeks turning red with embarrassment. "I just felt it was important that you knew where I stand."

"I appreciate that," I say. "We can discuss this further when things are less chaotic."

She laughs nervously. “Things *are* quite chaotic at the moment.”

I consider telling her about Blake, about the fact that his body is decomposing in that cabin, but I can’t bring myself to say the words. “Sometimes, I feel like I'm fighting against an invisible enemy,” I confess, staring out at the pitch-black ocean. “The cult's influence runs deep, and I don't know how far it goes.”

"Me neither," she says tightly.

Suddenly, there’s a noise, and I realize it’s the shuffling of feet.

My heart skips a beat as the sound of footsteps draws nearer. Gripping the railing tight, I turn to Molly. She looks just as scared. Her knuckles are white from clenching the metal.

“Come,” I tell her, yanking her toward a darkened corner. I shove her in. “Wait here.”

"Roger," she hisses, anxiety in her voice. “What are you doing?”

I take a step back, out into the light, and hold a finger to my lips. “Whatever it takes.”

43

Roger

Without a moment's hesitation, I step in front of Molly, shielding her from any potential threat. My heart pounds furiously in my chest, like a drummer rallying soldiers for battle.

I ready myself for attack, pure adrenaline guiding me.

A figure stumbles out of the shadows, gasping for breath as if he has just sprinted a great distance. I recognize him immediately. “Thomas?”

“Thank God,” he says. “I’ve been looking everywhere for you.”

His face is pale, his eyes wide with an unspoken terror that set my nerves on edge.

"Thomas?" Molly says, stepping out of the corner, her relief momentarily overpowering her worry. "What's wrong? You look like you've seen a ghost."

"Something...something terrible has happened," Thomas stammers. “You’re never gonna believe it.”

“Try me,” Molly says.

As Thomas looks at me, I feel a growing sense of foreboding tighten around my chest, threatening to suffocate me with its inescapable grip.

“What is it?” I urge, every fiber of my being demanding answers. I pray he’s not going to deliver bad news about Abby.

My jaw clenches. “Thomas?”

Struggling to catch his breath, he folds and places his hands on his knees. “Just give me a sec, okay?”

"Isaac...the cult," Thomas manages to choke out between labored breaths. "They've poisoned the bread. People are getting sick...dying."

Molly's hand flies to her mouth, stifling a gasp as she clutches my arm, her nails digging into my skin. The implications of Thomas’s words settling heavily in the pit of my stomach. The deck beneath them seems to sway, though whether it is due to the gentle rocking of the ship or the sheer weight of the information, I can’t be sure.

I can’t believe what I’m hearing.

"Are you certain?" I ask, struggling to maintain my composure.

“Pretty certain,” he says. “I was standing outside the kitchen, and I ran into my friend. I mean, he’s not my *real* friend, he’s crew, but we met on the first day and I always tipped him well so, anyway, he says he needs to tell me something. He said he needs to tell me the truth. He looked kind of confused, seeing as I’m wearing this cult shirt.”

“So, I crack a joke and then slipped him a twenty, and he confesses the cult is planning to sink the cruise ship because of their end of days beliefs, and that they had poisoned the bread with a toxin that was making many of the passengers sick and some of them die.”

I pinch the bride of my nose. “Fuck.”

Thomas looks from me to Molly. “My friend apologized, but he had to do what he was told. He warned me that if I didn't keep quiet about what he had told me, there would be consequences."

"He's not your friend," Molly says. "He just likes your money, and he doesn't want it to stop flowing in."

Thomas smirks. "Come on now, don't go spoiling the ending."

"So, anyway," Thomas continues, undeterred, "it felt like someone had sucked the air out of the room and my entire body was trembling. I stared at Joey—that's his name—unable to comprehend the magnitude of what I was being told."

"Is that it?" Molly quips. "That's all he said?"

"Pretty much, I mean, besides assuring me it was true. He just kept saying they're planning to sink the ship—and they've been poisoning the bread with a toxin that is slowly making the passengers sick. He said they won't die right away, but they will eventually succumb to the sickness."

"I felt like I was going to be sick listening to him," Thomas adds. "I had no idea what to do. I knew I had to do *something*, but I didn't know what. That's when I knew I had to find you."

I nod, understanding the gravity of the situation. I know we need to act fast, and we need to act smart. "This is exactly why they haven't come after us," I say. "They know we're going to die regardless—because they're poisoning us."

Molly purses her lips. "Sounds like their usual games."

Thomas nods vigorously, his eyes filled with an urgency that only serves to heighten the tension.

"God help us," Molly whispers, her voice barely audible above the wind. Her gaze meets mine, and in that instant, we both understood the gravity of our situation.

"Has anyone tried reasoning with Isaac about this?" I ask, my mind racing with possible courses of action. I only realize how stupid I sound once the words are out. What I'm really thinking is, I have to find my daughter. I am going to search every square inch of this ship until I find her, even if it gets me killed.

"Isaac flat-out refuses to help the sick," Molly says, her voice thick with disgust. "He's completely consumed by his twisted beliefs. It's like he's beyond reason."

Determination flashes in Thomas's eyes. "We can't just stand by and let innocent people die."

"Agreed," I say.

The three of us stand in the moonlit shadows, our faces a mixture of determination and fear. The rhythmic crashing of waves against the ship's hull serves as a haunting reminder of the urgency at hand.

"All right," I say, my jaw clenched. "Here's what I'm thinking—we can't just confront Isaac and his followers head-on—going to the bridge, that'd be a death wish. But we can't just do nothing, either. We need to investigate further, find out what they're planning and how to stop them. We need to search the ship."

Thomas's eyes dart nervously around the deck. "I think I know where they've been meeting. There's a storage room on the lower decks that's always locked. It would give them privacy, and nobody would think to look there."

"True," Molly says. "That can be our starting point. We'll go there tonight, steal their supplies, gather intel, whatever..."

My brow furrows with concern. I don't want to seem too eager. I don't want to drag them down with me, either, since my exploration is likely going to lead to trouble. "Before we do that, we need to warn people about the bread."

"I've tried telling people," Thomas says. "They didn't believe me. Just accused me of wanting it all for myself."

"Maybe..." I hesitate, my mind visibly working through the problem. "Maybe we could tamper with the bread supply itself—make it obvious that something's wrong with it, so people won't eat it."

"Smart thinking," Molly says. "We'll do that first, then move on to the storage room."

"Once we have what we need, we'll need to figure out how to

get control of the ship," I say, my thoughts racing ahead. "Breach the bridge, put out a distress call, anything to weaken their grip."

"Exactly," Thomas chimes in. "And maybe, if we're lucky, we can find some allies among the crew. Not everyone on this ship is part of Isaac's twisted cult."

"Okay," I say, my voice firm with resolve. "We have a plan. Better get to it."

"Stay alert," I remind them, my heart pounding in my chest. "Just be ready for anything."

"Of course," Molly says, her hand brushing against mine for a brief moment of comfort.

The deck is bathed in the eerie glow of the moon, casting elongated shadows that dance and flicker across the wooden planks. The salty sea breeze tugs at my clothes, as if urging me to turn back from the dangerous path from which we are about to embark. My heart hammers in my chest, and I swallow hard, forcing down the sickening mixture of fear and dread that threatens to overwhelm me.

"Are we ready for this?" Molly whispers, her eyes searching my face, searching for reassurance.

"Ready or not," I say, my voice steady despite the turmoil within me, "we have to act. There's no other choice."

"Remember," Thomas adds, his eyes scanning the deck, "we need to be careful. We don't know who we can trust."

As we step away from the railing and toward the darkened corridors of the ship, a blood-curdling scream echoes through the night, freezing us in our tracks. The chilling sound seems to originate from the deck below, reverberating off the walls like a macabre symphony.

"Dear God," Molly gasps, her hand flying to her mouth in horror. "What was that?"

"Trouble," I say grimly, my eyes narrowing as I try to pinpoint the source of the scream, sensing deep down that the real battle has just begun.

"Come on," Thomas urges, panic creeping into his voice. “Let’s see what’s up.”

The three of us exchange a look, understanding the gravity of the situation. With grim determination etched across our faces, the knowledge that time is running out propels us forward.

44

Roger

"Hey, Rog," Thomas whispers, his voice tense. "You all right?"

"Fine," I lie, forcing a smile that doesn't quite reach my eyes. Molly remains quiet, her grip tightening around the box cutter she's carrying.

As we draw nearer, a distraught crew member comes into view, standing in the doorway like a specter with her face pale and hands shaking. She's a young woman, barely out of her teens. Her uniform hangs off her body, as if the weight of the situation has caused her to shrink in on herself.

"Are you okay?" Molly asks softly, concern etched across her features.

The girl doesn't answer. Her gaze is locked onto something inside the cabin. Molly steps aside. I cautiously follow. Thomas on my heels. The air inside is thick with tension, and I have to resist the urge to gag on the horrible scent of decay.

I pull my shirt over my nose.

“It won’t help,” Molly says. “Just try not to breathe.”

"God almighty," I whisper, unable to tear my eyes away from the gruesome sight before us. Blake's lifeless body lies sprawled across the floor, dried blood splattered around his head like some twisted halo. His skin is unnaturally pale, and his vacant stare seems to bore into my soul.

"Jesus Christ," Molly gasps, as though she’s mocking me. If her voice wasn’t cracking under the strain, I’d think she was. "What the hell happened?"

"Looks like he was attacked," Thomas murmurs. “These are some sick people…”

I bite my lip, struggling to keep my composure. Obviously, I know what happened, but it's not something I'm ready to share. We're already dealing with enough secrets and lies; I can't bear to add my own to the growing pile.

Thomas, his face grim but determined, moves to console the distraught crew member, guiding her away from the gruesome scene.

"Come on," he murmurs to her, his voice soft and steady. "Let's get you out of here."

Watching them leave, I feel a strange mix of relief and guilt wash over me.

"Roger," Molly calls out as she scans the room, searching for any clues that might shed light on this grisly murder. Her gaze falls on a worn journal lying on the nightstand, its pages dog-eared and stained with ink. She picks it up hesitantly, flipping through the entries with a furrowed brow.

"Anything useful?" I ask, trying to keep my voice steady despite the pounding in my chest.

"I don't know yet... wait, listen to this." Molly's eyes widen as she reads the journal. I wait for her to say something, to explain what she’s looking at, but she doesn’t.

“Read it aloud,” I urge her, desperate for answers, but also terrified of what I might hear.

As Molly turns the next page, her face contorts into a grimace. "Oh God," she says, her voice quivering.

She looks up at me, wide-eyed. "This is Morgan's."

"Morgan? Who's Morgan?

"Your ex-wife."

"What do you mean?" My stomach turns over, knotting with anxiety. "How do you know my ex-wife?"

"She's the reason Abby was communicating with the cult. Abby wanted to locate Morgan."

"Jesus." I run my hands over my face as the weight of her words sinks in. "I knew she lived on some pot farm in the Northeast—I didn't think she'd joined a cult."

"She did live on a pot farm in the Northeast..."

"She was in a cult, though? That's what you're telling me?"

"That's what I'm telling you."

"I told Isaac—I tried to tell him—*no way* would she have just run off like that," she reveals, her words hanging heavy in the dimly lit cabin. "I just knew..."

"So where is she now?" I ask, but I know the answer. It just doesn't make any sense. There's no way this is possible, and yet, apparently, it's all right there in black and white.

Molly sighs. "I think this guy killed her."

I stagger back, feeling as though the wind has been knocked from my lungs, wondering if Molly has lost her mind. The room seems to tilt and sway around me, my hands clammy and my vision blurring at the edges. "I don't understand."

"Morgan worked on this ship. As a crew member. As Anna."

"Why would Morgan be using an alias?"

"Because Anna—or Morgan—was working for Isaac and the cult, scoping out the ship as a potential location," Molly continues, her voice shaking. "To celebrate the end of days."

"Morgan didn't believe in that kind of nonsense," I say with a scoff. "We lived together for more than a decade."

"She left this journal behind, detailing her time here and her interactions with the crew. But there are other entries, too. Some from Morgan's time at the farm."

My heart skips a beat at the mention of my ex-wife's name. I can feel the blood draining from my face, leaving me cold and numb. "There's just no way—Morgan wasn't the type to join a cult," I say, but even as the words roll off my tongue, I know it's a lie. By the time she walked out on us, I hardly knew her anymore.

"You knew her—Morgan?"

"Not really." Molly looks away. "No one really knows anyone when they get mixed up in this type of thing."

"Read it to me," I choke out.

"Are you sure?" Molly hesitates, her eyes full of concern. "He added entries… it's... gruesome."

"Please," I insist, needing to know the truth, no matter how painful it may be.

Molly takes a deep breath, steeling herself for what she's about to relay. Her voice trembles as she reads Blake's chilling account of the brutal murder.

"October 16th. She thought she was safe. Foolish woman. Anna, or should I say Morgan, was easy prey, right from the start. I didn't know if I'd actually go through with it, but I suppose we were both growing restless. I followed her into the bathroom, where the damp darkness clung to the walls like a shroud. She never even heard me coming. I struck her from behind, my blade slicing through the soft flesh of her throat."

My hands grip the edge of the table so tightly my knuckles turn ghost-white, the sharp sting of splinters digging into my palms a distant sensation compared to the agony tearing through my heart.

"Her blood sprayed across the shower, glistening like rubies against the porcelain. Her life slipped away as she gurgled and choked, her body convulsing with each desperate gasp for air. I watched the light fade from her eyes, the terror etched across her face a sight I'll never forget."

"Stop," I croak, unable to bear any more of the grisly details. "Please, just... stop."

Molly snaps the journal shut.

"Let's get back to it," I say, watching Molly pocket the journal. "We can deal with this later," I say, forcing my focus back to the task at hand.

"Back to it?" she says. "Roger, I think you're in shock. You can't just put everything off until later."

"Exactly. I need to find my daughter," I say, walking toward the door, not caring whether she follows.

As we leave the cabin, the shadows seem to close in around us, their darkness threatening to choke the very life from our lungs.

"Roger!" Molly cries out suddenly, her voice strangled with fear. "RUN!"

My heart leaps into my throat as I follow her gaze to the figure standing at the end of the corridor. As the faint light catches the glint of steel in his hand, one thing becomes clear: my nightmare is far from over.

45

Roger

"Where the hell is he getting all these bullets?" I mutter to myself as Molly and I sprint down the poorly lit corridor. Isaac's footsteps echo behind us like a twisted sonata of impending doom. I can almost feel the malice in each footfall, punctuated by the occasional gunshot.

"Less talking, more running!" Molly shouts, her voice strained but determined. The sharp crack of another gunshot rings out just as we narrowly dodge a bullet that grazes the wall beside me, sending sparks flying.

"Point taken," I rasp, my lungs burning for air, my legs feeling like they're about to give out at any moment. But there's no time to rest, not with Isaac hot on our heels. We reach a corner and make a split-second decision to duck into a supply closet, hoping it'll provide a temporary hiding spot. Molly clicks the door shut, careful not to make too much noise.

We press ourselves against the cold metal shelves, stocked with cleaning supplies and spare linen, trying to catch our breath while listening for any signs of Isaac's approach. The scent of bleach fills my nostrils, and I can't help but think it might be the last thing I ever smell.

"Roger," Molly whispers, her face pale but her eyes fierce, "if we don't make it out of this—"

"Hey, none of that talk now," I interrupt, forcing a grin onto my face despite the terror coursing through my veins.

"But, what if—"

"Then at least we went down fighting," I say, cutting her off once more.

She nods, and I can see the determination filling her eyes.

"Roger," Molly says, and I realize she's not just talking to me but also trying to calm herself down. "We've got this, right?"

"Yeah," I say, my heart pounding in my chest as I strain my ears for any sign of Isaac. "There's something very intriguing to me about not dying on this boat."

Molly glares at me and shakes her head. "I had no idea you were funny."

I can barely hear my own heartbeat over the blood rushing in my ears as we wait with bated breath. The seconds stretch out like taffy, until finally, Isaac's footsteps grow louder and closer, sending a shiver down my spine.

"Damn it, how does he always know where we are?" I think to myself, my gut clenched tight with anxiety. But then, as if by some miracle, Isaac's footsteps begin to fade away, growing fainter as he continues down the corridor.

"Let's go," Molly hisses, and I nod, offering her a half-grin that feels more like a grimace. We carefully crack open the door, peering out into the hallway before slipping out of our temporary sanctuary.

Which cabin was it last? 321? 459? I try to remember which one I stayed in last. I've been changing cabins nightly, a desperate attempt to avoid detection from Isaac and his cult. Problem is, it's gotten so convoluted that I can't even remember my own hiding place half the time. And with Abby potentially searching for me, I worry she won't be able to find me should she need to. If she's still alive, that is. And I have to believe she is, otherwise what's the point of this?

"Keep your wits about you," Molly reminds me as we stealthily make our way toward my current cabin. "Isaac is a lot of things, but he's not a quitter."

"Trust me, I haven't forgotten the fact that there's a gun-wielding maniac after us."

She smacks my arm. "Shh!"

Finally, we approach the cabin. I grip the box cutter in one hand and, with the other, I quickly scan the key card to unlock the door. The room is dark, the only illumination coming from the sliver of moonlight streaming through the balcony door. But as my eyes adjust, I realize we're not alone.

"Roger! Molly!" Thomas says, relief flooding his face as he emerges from the shadows. Around him, fourteen other passengers materialize, their expressions a mix of determination and worry.

Relief washes over me like a wave as I take in the sight of our makeshift crew. "Thomas, you have no idea how glad I am to see you."

"Likewise," he replies, his voice tense. "We need to talk."

"I know." I turn to address the group. "It's time to figure out what the hell we're going to do next."

As I look around at their determined faces, I can't help but feel a glimmer of hope. Maybe, just maybe, we stand a chance against Isaac and his deranged cult. But as I glance back toward the door, I can't shake the feeling that the worst is yet to come.

46

Roger

I rub at the sweat beading on my forehead, clearing my throat, before I share our recent encounter with Isaac. "So, Molly and I were sprinting down the corridor like a couple of lunatics, bullets practically nipping at our heels," I begin, voice dripping with sarcasm as I recount our harrowing escape.

"Isaac's getting more desperate by the minute," Molly adds, her voice shaking slightly. "He won't stop until he's hunted us all down."

The group exchanges worried glances. "It's now or never—we need to come up with a plan to take back control of the ship and put an end to this nightmare."

"Stealth is our best bet," Thomas suggests tentatively, his eyes darting from face to face. "If we can avoid detection, we might be able to outmaneuver Isaac and his followers."

"Or we could go in guns blazing," another passenger chimes in, earning a few raised eyebrows. "They won't expect us to fight back with such force."

A murmur of disagreement ripples through the group, and I can feel the tension mounting as the debate heats up. My fingers twitch nervously at my sides, and I unconsciously clench and unclench my fists.

"Only one problem," I say. "We don't have guns. But don't worry, it gets worse—it's very clear now; they do."

"How'd they get guns on the ship?" the elderly woman demands.

"Crew, probably," the man next to her answers. "They can load whatever they want."

"I don't think it works that way," she scoffs. "Besides, I saw those bomb-sniffing dogs when we boarded the ship."

"Look lady," he snaps. "You look old enough to understand the way the world works—slip someone enough Benjamins, they'll look away."

She shakes her head. "People these days, they've lost their morals. What a shame."

"Yeah," the man huffs. "Now, we gotta go kill people…with just our morals, because we don't have guns."

The lady grins. "I'm very good with knives. You wanna see?"

"Look," Molly interjects, her voice rising in intensity. "We can argue strategy all night, but the fact remains that these people"—she spits the word like it's venom—"are dangerous. They've taken control of the ship, and they're not afraid to kill anyone who stands in their way."

Her words hang heavy in the air, and I can see the resolve hardening on everyone's faces.

"Maybe we can combine both strategies," I suggest, trying to ease the growing tension in the room. "Who here has any experience in combat or self-defense?" I ask, raising an eyebrow.

A few hands go up, including the old woman's.

"All right, we'll be on the aggressive team. Everyone else will focus on stealth."

"Sounds good," Molly agrees. "Now, let's gather the weapons."

A murmur of agreement circulates among the group, and I can't help but feel a sense of pride swelling in my chest. We may be a motley crew, but we're united in our determination to take down Isaac and his twisted cult.

Molly calls from the other side of the room. "Found some kitchen knives!"

I smile big, even though I've only found the minibar.

She cranes her head in my direction. "See if you can find anything else that might work as a weapon."

"Roger that," I mutter, unable to resist the pun. My attempt at humor falls flat, though, and I pivot my attention back to the task at hand.

"All right," I say, steeling myself for the battle ahead. "Let's get to work."

As we complete our plans and prepare for the fight of our lives, I can't help but think of Abby out there somewhere, hopefully recovering, potentially searching for me. I pray that she's safe, and that we'll have the chance to reunite once this madness is over.

"Time's ticking away," Thomas reminds me, glancing at the tiny whiskey bottles I have lined up and then at his watch. "We need to move now."

"I'm aware," I say, because it's true. The clock on the wall taunts me, its hands inching closer and closer to 3:00 a.m. The tension in the room is thick enough to cut with one of our stolen kitchen knives. As each second ticks by, I can feel my heart rate accelerate, pounding a frantic rhythm against my ribcage.

"All right, everyone," I call out, my voice strained. "Let's huddle up for a moment."

The group shuffles closer together, their eyes wide and alert. I look around at these people—strangers who have become allies—and try to muster up confidence.

"We all know the stakes here," I say, my words tinged with a hint of sarcasm that I hope masks my growing uncertainty. "But we're stronger together, and if there's any chance in hell we're going to pull this off, it's by working as one."

A murmur of agreement ripples through the group.

"Remember," Thomas adds, his voice low and steady, "we need to stick together. And most importantly, we need to believe in ourselves."

"Here's to taking back the ship," Molly says fiercely, her eyes shining with determination. She holds up a steak knife like a toast, and we all raise our makeshift weapons in solidarity.

"Cheers to that." I force a grin that doesn't quite reach my eyes. "Now, let's get ready to move."

"Roger," Molly whispers, her hand coming to rest on my shoulder. "It's going to be fine."

"Thanks, Molly." I offer a weak smile. "I hope you're right."

With one last shared glance of determination, I lead my team toward the door. My heart threatens to burst from my chest as I grasp the handle, and I can almost feel the darkness lurking just beyond, waiting to swallow us whole.

"Ready?" My voice is barely audible over the pounding in my ears. The others nod, their faces set with grim resolve.

"Let's do this," I say, and as I open the door, we step into the night, unsure of what horrors await us on the other side.

47

Roger

The moment our feet hit the warm, damp deck, I can feel the weight of darkness pressing upon us. The moon hovers above, a pale sliver in the sky, casting eerie shadows. A shiver runs down my spine as the wind murmurs through the deck like a chorus of disembodied voices.

"Stick to the shadows," I whisper. "Otherwise we're dead."

"Roger, focus," Molly hisses, her eyes locked on our surroundings. "We need to stay sharp."

"Right," I mutter, shaking off my unease and mentally berating myself for letting fear creep in. "Sharp as our box cutters."

She gasps as the realization sets in. "Are you drunk?"

I shrug. "Maybe a little."

"Seriously?"

"What?" I say. "Who wants to die sober?"

"Well, I don't want to die at all."

“Whiskey lowers my inhibitions. I’m a better shot with a little warmth in my belly. Trust me.”

Molly doesn’t answer, which is good because when you’re planning a sneak attack, it helps if you’re not asking stupid questions.

We move carefully, our footsteps as silent as possible, while every creak and groan of the ship sets my nerves on edge. I can't help but imagine Isaac and his cult lurking in every corner, waiting to pounce. It's taking every ounce of self-control not to let my paranoia get the better of me.

"Did you hear that?" Thomas says, causing us all to freeze in our tracks.

"Could just be the ship settling," I suggest, trying to keep the tremor from my voice. "Or, you know, something much worse."

"Let's keep moving," Molly says firmly.

As we continue our stealthy advance, I can't help but reflect on the absurdity of our situation. Here we are, a motley group of passengers, armed with little more than kitchen utensils, attempting to overthrow a murderous cult on a luxury cruise liner. It would almost be hilarious if it weren't so terrifying.

"All right, Team Stealth—we're almost to the bridge. Remember, stay quiet and stay hidden."

Thomas’s face is set with determination. “Copy that.”

“Godspeed.” I watch as our two teams split up, each heading down a separate corridor. My heart pounds in my chest like a jackhammer, and I can't shake the feeling that we're being watched.

As we inch closer to the bridge, the ship seems to grow darker, more oppressive somehow. The air feels thick and suffocating, coating my throat with each labored breath. It's as if the very atmosphere is conspiring against us, trying to smother our rebellion before it has a chance to ignite.

"Roger," Molly hisses, her eyes wide with fear. "Do you feel that?"

My pulse quickening as I scan the darkness for any signs of danger. “Feel what?”

"Like... something's about to happen," she says, her voice trembling. "Something terrible."

"Maybe it's just nerves," I suggest, though I can't deny the growing unease that gnaws at my gut. "Or maybe it's the fact that we're about to walk into a nest of homicidal maniacs armed with nothing but cutlery."

"God, Roger, not now," Molly snaps, her frustration momentarily overriding her terror. "We have to keep going."

“Right.” I swallow hard. "No turning back now."

As we round the corner, our path is suddenly bathed in a sickly green light that spills from beneath a nearby door. My heart leaps into my throat, and I can't suppress a gasp at the sight that greets us.

"Good lord," I choke out, staring in horror at the scene before us. "What the hell is happening here?"

And then, just as the first panicked screams begin to echo through the ship, I realize we may already be too late.

48

Roger

The sea roars in a frenzy, waves smashing against the ship's hull like a thunderous beast. I feel the floor shifting and groaning beneath me as the vessel is thrashed around in the storm.

Molly holds her stomach, eyes clenched shut, struggling to keep her lunch down. Everyone looks a little green—not from the light. This is not ideal for a cruise ship rebellion.

Thomas hisses over the din, determination rolling off him. "Damn it all."

We huddle together outside the bridge, casting glances toward our companions: vacationers-turned-warriors, armed with whatever they could scavenge—broken bottles, fire extinguishers, even golf clubs.

The eerie green light intensifies, casting a sickly glow at our feet. *What kind of twisted games are these cultists playing?*

"Stay sharp," Thomas warns. "There's no telling what we'll find in there."

"Or who," Molly adds, a shiver of fear flickering across her face.

"Whatever it is," I say, clenching my jaw, "we're not backing down now."

I take a deep breath and kick open the door with one swift, powerful motion. We're met with a scene straight out of a horror film.

Luke and Jacob are bound and gagged, their faces twisted with terror and agony, surrounded by cult members conducting some diabolical ritual. The green light turns out to be a strobe light they must have stolen from the ship's theater. It flickers chaotically, throwing dreadful shadows on the walls like they're underlining the abhorrence of what we're witnessing. The cult has transformed it into a carnival of pain and human sacrifice, and I can't help but shudder at how close Molly and I came to being part of this nauseating display. Fear for Abby tears through me.

The smell of blood hangs heavy in the air, mixed with the salt-laced sea breeze that slips in through the gaps in the bridge. My heart feels like it's trying to hurl itself out of my ribcage, as if desperate to escape from this horror show. I can almost taste fear and desperation—bitter on my tongue.

"Enough!" Molly screams, her voice strained and soaked with anger. She charges forward, her eyes fixed on Isaac, the madman who masterminded this abominable scene. For a second, time appears to slow down as she lunges toward the cult members nearest Luke and Jacob, a knife raised high overhead.

Molly cries out, her voice raw and strong. “Get in here, you bastards!”

That's our cue. The rest of them rush forward like an ocean wave of retribution. As they collide with the cultists, their box cutters and steak knives glinting cruelly under the strobe light, I'm struck by how unbelievably surreal all this is.

"Watch your back, Roger!" Thomas shouts, the words barely audible above the chaos of grunts, curses, and the stomach-churning sound of metal on flesh. I spin just in time to dodge a wild swing from a cult member, her face distorted into a grotesque mask of rage.

"Thanks," I grunt, counter-attacking with the crowbar I'd snatched from the ship's maintenance closet. Her knife clatters onto the floor as I slam the crowbar down on her arm, her agonized howl ringing in my ears.

The fight is brutal, chaotic, and terrifyingly intimate. There's no room for finesse here, only raw survival instinct. The air is thick with the smell of sweat and blood, a coppery tang that coats the back of my throat. I can feel the vibrations of each desperate blow as it connects with bone and muscle, and the heat of the bodies around me is suffocating.

"Get them off me!" Luke screams, his voice muffled by the gag hanging half out of his mouth. Molly has managed to reach him and Jacob, her eyes wild with terror and determination as she fights to free them from their bonds. Their captors snarl and lash out like cornered animals, but Molly's resolve is unwavering.

"Almost got it," she pants through clenched teeth, her fingers slick with blood as she works at the knots. "Just hang on!"

Thomas's hoarse yell snaps me back to reality, "Roger! Behind you!"

49

Roger

My stomach churns as the cruise ship bucks and rolls, but I have bigger concerns. I lock eyes with a cult member charging at me, brandishing a knife like it's Excalibur—clearly, he's not one to appreciate the finer points of swordsmanship. Regardless, I don't have time for an impromptu history lesson.

I barrel toward my attacker. He swings blindly, but I duck under his arm and grab it, wrenching the blade from his grip and kicking it away. He lunges for me again, arms swinging wildly. A swift knee to the gut stops him in his tracks and bends him double, gasping for breath.

I'm about to finish him when the elderly lady shouts, "Roger, on your left!"

I spin, narrowly avoiding another knife. The cultist is grinning like a madman, but I'm not about to let him enjoy this. I raise the crowbar, swinging it like a bat at his head. The grin vanishes as he crumples to the ground, senseless. That's three down, too many more to go.

A fourth cultist approaches, her eyes vacant and empty—or maybe that's just the green strobe light playing tricks on me. She holds a steak knife like she thinks it's going to save her life, but I know better: with one swift movement, I disarm her and headbutt her into submission.

Adrenaline races through my veins as I taunt them. "Come on, fuckers! Is that all you've got?"

Molly screams my name, terror dripping from every syllable. "There are more of them coming!"

"Great," I say, gritting my teeth. "Just what we need."

The reinforcements pour into the bridge like a tidal wave of darkness, their twisted faces illuminated by the green strobe light. My heart pounds in my chest, but I refuse to let fear take root.

I catch sight of Isaac, his eyes wild with panic as he watches his followers crumble before the might of our little rebellion. He grits his teeth, his face contorted in rage, and shouts an order that sends a shiver down my spine.

"Burn this ship to the ground! Start in the engine room and burn it all!" Isaac roars, desperation seeping into every word.

Determined not to let Isaac's maniacal plan succeed, I bulldoze through cultists and rebels alike, the floor slick with blood under my feet. I know that if a fire starts in the engine room, there's no saving this ship or its passengers; they've disabled the life boats. We've tried and tried, with no luck. We'll all become sacrifices to whatever twisted god these psychos worship.

Molly calls after me, agony punctuating her question. "Where are you going?"

I can't risk a glance in her direction. "I'm stopping these lunatics from setting the ship on fire!"

But I never do reach the engine room, I'm tackled from behind, my heart lurching into my throat. I struggle against the iron grip, but it's no use. My neck twists around to see Isaac glowering at me, his eyes filled with madness and rage.

I'm trapped.

50

Roger

"Thought you could stop me, did you?" Isaac sneers, his breath hot on my face. "You've been a problem from the start, but now it ends."

I refuse to give him the satisfaction of seeing me waver. "Go to hell."

"Maybe I will." His mouth forms a twisted grin. "But not before you."

And just like that, the world slows to a crawl, the screams and clashes around us fading into the background.

I focus on the pulsating vein in Isaac's temple, beating like a metronome to the chaotic symphony around us. The heat is suffocating with smells of sweat, fear, and blood. It burns my nostrils with each breath. There's a certain irony in this moment—the maniac who has hijacked this cruise ship is now holding me hostage. How this plays out makes all the difference. Not just for me, but for everyone. I would laugh if it weren't for the fact that I'm inches away from death.

“Ah, Roger,” he purrs with perverse pleasure. "Finally got you right where I want you."

"Congratulations. You must be so proud."

My heart races, but I refuse to let him see how terrified I am. "Quick question: Is this your idea of a vacation? Because I can assure you there are better ways to spend your time at sea."

Isaac presses the cold steel of his blade against my throat, drawing a thin line of blood. "You have no idea what we're trying to achieve here, do you?"

"Nope," I admit, wincing as the pain intensifies. "But I doubt it's worth all the trouble you've gone through."

"Your ignorance will be your undoing," he snarls, tightening his grip on me. I try to swallow, but the pressure on my throat makes it impossible.

"Roger!" Molly screams over the chaos, her voice desperate and pleading. She's still fighting off cult members, her face bathed in blood and grime. Our eyes lock, and for a split-second, it feels like time has stopped.

"Enough of this!" Isaac bellows, the patience draining from his voice. He drags me toward the a door, the blade pressed against my neck. "You're coming with me, and if anyone tries to follow, they'll pay for it with your life."

I mumble a curse under my breath as we approach the door.

The noise from outside gradually fades away as Isaac shoves me inside the room. I stumble forward, nearly crashing into one of the metal pipes snaking across the floor.

"Welcome to the belly of the beast." He tightens his grip around my arm. "This is where the real magic happens."

I take in the maze of wires and piping, feeling like I've stepped into some kind of mechanical jungle with no clear path to follow. "So what now?" I murmur, trying to maintain an air of calmness.

"Now we wait," Isaac says with a malicious grin, his eyes

gleaming with madness and triumph. "The final stage of our plan is about to unfold, and you'll witness it firsthand."

I feel sweat trickling down my back and hear blood rushing in my ears. Every breath feels like it could be my last, but I stand tall, staring straight into Isaac's eyes. "You know," I say carefully, choosing each word with precision. "I've been thinking about what you said earlier."

"Oh?" He raises an eyebrow, intrigued. "And what's that?"

"You said my ignorance will be my undoing," I repeat, my voice steady despite the fear roiling inside me. "But isn't it possible that your arrogance will be yours?"

Isaac's grin fades, replaced by a scowl. "What are you talking about?"

"I'm talking about the fact that you're so convinced you're right, so convinced you're the hero of your own story, that you can't see the damage you're causing," I say, hoping to get under his skin. "You've killed innocent people. You've caused chaos and destruction. And for what? Some misguided sense of purpose?"

Isaac's grip on me tightens, his eyes filling with rage. "You have no idea what we're trying to achieve here," he growls. "But you'll see soon enough."

"I don't need proof to know that what you are doing is wrong," I declare with increasing defiance in my voice. "You're nothing but a delusional psychopath, and you'll eventually get what's coming to you."

Isaac's face contorts with fury, and for a moment, I think he's going to kill me right then and there. But then, a strange look crosses his face, almost like he's considering something.

"You know what, Roger?" he says, his voice low and dangerous. "You're right. I am the hero of my own story. And in my story, the hero doesn't lose." With that, he raises his blade, ready to strike.

I close my eyes, bracing for the impact. But then I hear a sudden commotion outside. Shouts and gunshots ring out, and for a moment, I think help has finally arrived.

Isaac hesitates, his attention momentarily diverted. That's all the opening I need. With a sudden burst of strength, I elbow him in the gut and break free of his grip. I stumble backward, nearly tripping over a loose pipe.

The two of us grapple, each fighting for control. The air is thick with the scent of sweat and metal, the sound of our labored breathing and the clanging of machinery drowning out everything else.

And then, just as suddenly as it began, it's over. There's a sickening crunch as Isaac's head collides with one of the pipes, and he crumples to the ground. I seize the knife. He looks up at me wild-eyed and he begs, "Please."

I punch him in the nose with my free hand. "Say it again."

"Please!" he shrieks. "Don't—"

"Fuck off," I say and then I slit his throat without hesitation.

For a long moment, I just stand there, trying to catch my breath. I've survived, but the battle is far from over. Isaac isn't the only maniac on this boat, and he won't be the last.

51

Roger

My hands still stained with blood, I rush back to the bridge. Isaac's face forever burned in my mind. I burst through the doors onto the deck of the ship, where a cacophony of noise and light replaces the darkness and hum of machinery. The wind blares around me as if mocking my futile attempts at regaining control.

"I'm outta here," the elderly woman, Darlene, grunts, surprising me with her agility as she inflates a life raft she tells me she found in the captain's quarters. "This ship's cursed."

I can't help but feel a pang of admiration—even envy—for her determination. She jumps overboard without a second thought and I contemplate following suit, letting the icy embrace of the ocean take me rather than face whatever is waiting for us on this godforsaken vessel. But I shake that thought away just as quickly as it came; I have no time for cowardice.

"Roger!" Molly calls out, "Good, you're back."

"You mean I'm alive."

Her fingers skitter across the communication controls with precision, fueled only by adrenaline. "I'm trying to send out an SOS signal."

My heart races as I watch her work, hoping against hope that someone will hear our plea for help. But deep down, a dark voice whispers that we're already too far gone, that there's no saving any of us from the nightmare unfolding on this ship. I shake my head, desperate to silence the pessimistic thoughts threatening to consume me.

"Come on, come on," Molly mutters under her breath. "Work, damn it."

I can only stand there feeling helpless and useless as I watch her struggle with the bullet-riddled communication system. My fingers twitch, itching to do something—anything—to help.

Suddenly, a flash of relief flickers over Molly's face. "Got it! I think it went through!"

"Thank God," I gasp in disbelief as a wave of relief washes over me. The metallic tang of adrenaline lingers in my mouth and my hands tremble, but I still take a step back from the bridge and leave Molly to her work. The ship groans around us like an injured animal, and the icy ocean wind freezes my skin.

"Roger!" A voice snaps me back to the here and now. Thomas, looking like a military officer in his bearing, strides toward me with icy determination, two guns in his possession. I watch as other passengers follow suit, fueled by a newfound courage and determination, effectively neutralizing the threat posed by the remaining cult members. If there's one thing that can bring people together, it's apparently the threat of imminent death.

Thomas barks an order, gesturing to the disarmed cultists. Hidden rage simmers beneath his controlled facade.

"Help me round them up," he says.

I nod and find myself inspired by his level-headedness amid the chaos. We move together toward the main dining hall, herding the defeated cult members like lost sheep and forcing them to sit and remain under watch. They look broken and confused now; a dark chuckle forms deep in my chest. Not so powerful now, are they?

Thomas's gaze scans the group, his voice low and commanding. "Keep an eye on them. I'll make sure the perimeter is secure."

My heart races, but my voice remains strong. "Got it."

The instant he disappears from view, I study the faces of our captives. Some wear expressions of fear, others defiance, but all of them are undeniably human. It's a sobering thought—how easily the line between "us" and "them" can blur.

"Please," one of the cult members whispers. "We didn't want this."

"You didn't want it?" I sneer, unable to contain my bitterness. "Your actions sure showed something different."

My gaze locks with hers, and in an instant I can see something in her eyes—regret? Fear? It's impossible to tell, and really doesn't matter.

"Make yourselves at home," I snarl, glowering at the cultists. "I have a feeling we might be here for a while."

I turn away from them, thoughts of Molly racing through my mind. She's up on the bridge somewhere, still sending out her SOS call. The tension that hangs in the air is so thick it feels like it could choke us all.

"Roger," Thomas urges as he returns, his face etched with worry. "We have a problem."

"Another one?"

"Isaac's body is missing," he says, his eyes darting around the room as if expecting it to appear any second now.

"Missing? How does a body just disappear?"

"Beats me."

Molly steps forward, her expression a mix of relief and anxiety. "More importantly," she says coolly, "ask me about the SOS call."

Thomas and I look at her expectantly.

“Got a response,” she confirms. "And now we wait."

52

Roger

Waiting is not my specialty, but there are times when it's necessary. Like now, for instance. Molly and I exchange a glance that says more than any words ever could about the courage and strength we've both gained in this chaos. A bond forged through shared adversity, or just desperate necessity—either way, it's not important now.

"Once things settle down," I say, "I'm going to search for Abby." I can tell Molly is expecting me to say something else, but I can't bring myself to say it. The mention of Abby brings a flicker of concern to Molly's eyes, and she gives me a slight nod before musing, "But maybe we should test the intercom system first—see if it's functional."

"Good idea." I nod, glancing at the increasing number of innocent passengers gathering in the restaurant. Word has spread quickly, and their presence bolsters our numbers, improving our chances of success. We work together to secure the restaurant, barricading doors and windows to prevent any cult members from escaping or receiving reinforcements.

"Maybe we can use the intercom to communicate with the rest of the ship," suggests Molly. "Let them know what's happening. Coordinate our efforts."

"Assuming anyone left on board is still alive," I add, unable to suppress the skeptic in me.

She rolls her eyes. "Thanks for the vote of confidence."

"It's not you," I say, giving her a halfhearted smile. Truth is, I've seen too much horror in the past hours to have much faith left.

Molly strides up to the intercom panel and drills her finger into the buttons, sparking life into the dormant system. A spark of electricity crackles through the air, followed by a soft hum.

"Hello?" Molly's voice echoes through the restaurant, amplified and distorted by the intercom. "Is anyone out there?"

"Guess we'll wait and see," I say, studying the faces of the surrounding passengers. Fear and uncertainty are etched into every line, every wrinkle—but so, too, is determination.

"They're going to kill us, you know," a cultist keeps saying to anyone who will listen. "We are all going to die..."

"Please," a timid voice reaches my ears, "can you turn on some music? Something soothing?"

"Sure," I say, my lips twisting into a smile that's more grimace than anything else. "Anyone got a playlist for surviving a group of fanatics?"

"Hilarious," Molly replies, but there's an edge to her voice. The stakes are too high for humor now, and we all know it.

My eyes sweep over the huddled passengers, their whispered conversations growing louder, more frantic. Tensions are at a boiling point—I can practically see the steam rising from their furrowed brows.

"Look!" A woman with wild hair and war paint smeared across

her cheeks slams a fist onto the makeshift barricade. "We can't just sit here like sitting ducks! We need to fight back! We need to kill them all!"

"Are you insane?" a middle-aged man in a stained Hawaiian shirt retorts. "We're not equipped for that. It'd be suicide."

"Better than waiting to die," the woman snarls, her eyes burning with hatred.

"Enough." Thomas steps between them, his voice carrying the weight of authority. "Arguing won't get us anywhere."

"Help," Molly says, her hand trembling as she clutches the intercom, "will come. We just need to sit tight. Killing them will not solve your problems, believe me."

"Easy for you to say," the war-painted woman spits. "You weren't there when they took my brother."

"Neither were you," I say to the lady, which is more of a projection than anything else. "Or he might still be alive."

Molly's eyes widen in shock and concern. "Roger," she says firmly. "Don't."

"Sorry," I shake my head, regret gnawing at my gut. "I didn't mean..."

"His daughter is still missing," Molly explains sadly.

"Apology," the woman replies, her voice strained, "not accepted."

In the hallway just outside the doors, voices clamor for blood and justice—vengeance for what the cult has done. The noise crescendos until it seems to shake the walls of the restaurant. We can hear each angry word like a physical force, pounding against our eardrums.

"Wait," a voice cuts through the air, high-pitched and trembling. "Look!"

We turn as one, our gazes drawn to the windows, and there, on the horizon, a Coast Guard ship slices through the water, its hull gleaming like a beacon of salvation.

Molly breathes out a tearful “Thank God” as the room erupts into cheers and cries of relief. "We're saved!"

I keep my eyes fixed on the approaching vessel, my heart caught between hope and dread. "Maybe," I mutter, as an ominous wave of questions wash over me. "Or maybe this is just the beginning of something else."

53

Abby

My eyes snap open, and the smell of lavender and chamomile wafts into my nostrils. Soft, ambient music plays like a lullaby in the background, offering a brief respite from the horrific reality surrounding me.

The ship's spa has been transformed into a makeshift recovery room for me, and although my body aches with pain, I'm thankful for this small sanctuary.

Dimmed lights cast a warm glow on the wooden walls, and plush towels are carefully folded on shelves, their whiteness seeming so pure amid all the chaos. The calming atmosphere is almost enough to make me forget the bloodshed that stains the rest of the ship.

Remember to breathe, I whisper to myself, trying to keep the panic under control. I'm not sure if the tranquil environment is helping or if it's simply the pain meds coursing through my veins —but I'll take what I can get.

The door creaks open, and hushed voices creep into the room. Jacob and Luke, whose bodies are covered in ugly bruises and gashes, creep tentatively inside, seeking medical attention.

"Dr. Clifford," Jacob murmurs, his voice strained. "The passengers have taken the ship back, for now."

Luke chimes in, his voice cracking under the weight of his exhaustion. "Not just for now—we spotted a Coast Guard ship on the horizon. They'll be aboard soon."

The doctor, an older man with kind gray eyes, nods solemnly as he assesses their injuries. He works quietly but efficiently, aware of the urgency of our situation. The tension in the room is palpable, and I can't help but hold my breath, hoping that this nightmare will soon end.

Lying there, I pick apart their words for hidden truths and meanings. My mind races with questions—how did they defeat them? Is it true? Where's Dad? Is this the end or just a brief reprieve?

Focus on the present, just the next breath, I tell myself, pushing back dark thoughts trying to consume me. For now, all that matters is that rescue is imminent—and somehow, against all odds, we're going to be okay. I smile, realizing how much I sound like Dad.

But it's Jacob's smile that swims in front of me as I drift back into a restless, medicated sleep.

When I wake, the doctor's gentle hands are working meticulously on Luke. His face contorts in pain, and I strain to hear any snippets of conversation about our rescue. Then I hear Dad's name in hushed tones.

"Roger," Jacob whispers through gritted teeth, "he's holding them in the restaurant."

"Is he okay?" I ask, my voice trembling like a fragile branch in a storm.

The doctor looks up at me with sympathetic eyes and says,

"Your dad is safe, Abby, he'll be here soon." He pauses his stitching before adding, "Just rest for now."

I nod, trying to suppress the worry gnawing at the edges of my mind. I can't shake the feeling that Dad's safety might be ephemeral; that things could shift in an instant.

I don't remember what they say, or what happens after that. My eyes flutter open, and the edges between reality and sleep blur. But I do know that when the spa door swings open, and there he stands—my father—I feel happier than I've ever felt in my whole life.

I also know that if I die, *this* was enough. Seeing his face had been all that mattered. It's the only thing I've been hanging on for. I want to apologize for everything. For dragging him on this ship—for lying about the reason we are here. For making him feel like he isn't enough—like I need Morgan in order to be happy, to feel complete.

"Dad," I choke out as tears prick my eyes. "I'm so sorry."

His face is a mixture of relief and concern as he rushes over to my side. "Abby," he murmurs, his voice thick with emotion. "My God—"

As he holds me, the room fades away—the doctor's quiet ministrations, Jacob and Luke's clipped conversations. Even the lingering scent of lavender, antiseptic, and fear seem to vanish. For a moment, it's just us and nothing else matters.

But then an urgent knock on the door interrupts our moment, and a man's voice pierces through the air: "Coast Guard's here! They're boarding now!"

Relief floods through me like a tidal wave as I imagine the ship teeming with men and women in uniform, ready to rescue us from this nightmare.

Suddenly, the door swings open and a battalion of Coast Guard officers strides in, their authoritative presence both calming and intimidating.

"Are we all accounted for?" one of them barks out, his eyes scouring the room.

"Abby, her father, Jacob, Luke, and myself," the doctor utters, pointing each one of us out. "We're all ready to go."

"Fine, hang tight," the officer instructs, his voice stern yet reassuring. "Medics are on their way; prepare for evacuation."

54

Roger

I stand on the deck of the rescue ship, a salty breeze whipping around me. Coast Guard officers rush around, helping survivors from the cruise liner. The sun beats down on my face, and I feel unsteady on my feet, a bone-deep exhaustion. The noise of those around us fades away, and the only sound is our hearts pounding.

Abby lies on a stretcher, eyes distant as she takes in the scene before us. "Hard to believe it's over," she murmurs. It's been one hell of a ride, both physically and emotionally—but she doesn't need me to say that out loud.

I place a hand on her shoulder and feel her tense body beneath my touch. Her gaze meets mine, and we share a knowing look.

"Time to say goodbye, I guess," she murmurs, her voice cracking slightly as she looks around at the faces of those who have shared this twisted journey with us.

We exchanged contact information with some of the other passengers, promising to keep in touch despite the uncertainty of the future. The weight of these hastily scribbled numbers seems heavier than any anchor, grounding us to this unforgettable experience.

Jenna is the outlier. She pulls me aside; says she wants to disappear for awhile. She asks me not to mention anything about her and Blake. “I want to put this all behind me,” she says. “I’m in my own kind of trouble, I don’t need more—you understand?”

“Of course.”

She pulls me into an awkward hug and then I watch her walk away.

“She okay?” Thomas asks, striding up.

“I think so.”

“Good.” Thomas grabs my hand in his, tears rimming his eyes. "Take care of yourself," he says and then adds, nodding to Abby: "And take care of her."

I promise him I will and quickly break away from the embrace.

As we await our transport flight, Abby gazes one last time at the cruise ship that has been both our prison and our sanctuary, a mix of relief and sadness washing over her like waves crashing against its hull.

"Let's go home," she whispers, her voice almost drowned out by the seagulls overhead. I nod in agreement, understanding the weight of her words.

I take her hand. “Home it is.”

She looks up at me, desperation in her eyes. “Promise me something?”

“Sure.”

“Promise you'll call Molly when we get to the hospital.”

"I will," I tell her. “Who else is gonna believe our stories after this hellish ‘vacation?’”

Abby narrows her eyes. “Where is she, anyway?”

“She’s tied up with the authorities. We spoke briefly.”

A small smile flits across her lips, even though tears glint in her eye. “I mean it, Dad—about calling her.”

“I mean it, too,” I say. “I already told her I would.”

“It's just... I don't want to lose this connection we have with her —with any of them…”

"Neither do I," I admit, feeling a lump forming in my throat. "But we have each other, and that's what matters most."

I glance back at the motley parade of survivors, each bearing their own invisible scars from the horrors they've endured aboard the ship. The salty sea breeze fills my nostrils and hope blossoms inside me as the sun's rays wash over us. For a moment, the horrors of life on board are forgotten.

“It's going to feel so good to be back on solid ground,” Abby murmurs, her voice tinged with relief.

"Never thought I'd appreciate concrete that much," I quip, eager to feel the sturdiness beneath my feet.

We watch as the other passengers converse, some with tearful goodbyes, others with stoic nods of acknowledgment. Each of them, like us, is forever changed by their time on the ship, and I can't help but wonder what lies ahead for all of us.

"Roger," Abby says, her eyes locked with mine. "Promise me one last thing..."

"Anything," I answer without a moment's hesitation.

"Promise you won't let me step foot on a boat again."

"That," I tell her, “I can guarantee.”

"Thank you, Dad," she says earnestly as they wheel her toward the waiting helicopter. She squeezes my hand tight. "Thanks for everything. And I'm sorry this trip was far from what we wanted it to be—"

"Hey," I joke, trying to brighten the mood. "At least we've got one heck of a story to tell at parties, right?"

"Dad!" She acts horrified. "How can you even joke about that?"

"Because sometimes, Abby, it's all we've got."

55

Abby

The aroma of sizzling bacon and freshly brewed coffee mingles with the clatter of dishes, creating a symphony of sound and smell that is Lucky's Diner. It's been a year since my rescue from the cruise ship, and I take comfort in the bustling atmosphere of this place. Before our hellish "vacation," Roger never would have let me work, especially not in the middle of a pandemic, and especially such a labor intensive job.

But everything is different now. I refuse to let this disease rule my life, and we mainly only get takeout orders, anyway. As I wipe down a counter, I take a moment to appreciate the way sunlight filters through the grease-smeared windows, casting an amber glow over the chipped Formica countertops.

"Order up!" the cook shouts, placing a plate of steaming pancakes on the counter. I'm boxing them up when I glance over to see a familiar figure enter the diner amid the chaos—Jacob.

His eyes sweep the room until they lock onto mine, and his

face breaks into a warm smile that sends a flutter through my chest. It's been a long time since I've felt something so simple as this kind of happiness. He strides over, effortlessly navigating the narrow gaps between tables, and I can't help but grin as I greet him.

"Jacob! What are you doing here?" My voice is an octave higher than usual, betraying my excitement.

"Coming to see you, obviously," he says, his smile widening as he takes me in. "You look great. This place suits you."

"Thanks." I feel my cheeks flushing at the unexpected compliment. "I guess there's something about the smell of bacon grease that really brings out my inner glow."

He chuckles, and there's a fleeting moment where it feels like the past year never even existed. Suddenly, the air crackles with anticipation, and I revel in its electricity.

Jacob perches on a stool at the counter, his gaze fixated on me as I hand him a menu. "What's good here?" he asks.

"That depends on how daring you're feeling," I reply, handing him the laminated sheet. "But if you want my personal recommendation, the 'Heart Attack Special' is a death-defying feat of culinary expertise."

A smile quirks on Jacob's lips. "I'm up for the challenge."

"Excellent choice." I scribble down his order and slide it into the kitchen window before leaning against the counter, the cool metal pressing into my hip. "So, I take it Roger called?"

"Um, yes, actually," Jacob responds, rubbing the back of his neck. "He said he was going on a hunting trip with Molly. That's why I'm here."

"That doesn't sound like Dad at all," I mutter under my breath. "Seriously, he knows you're here?"

"I think it was Molly's idea. But he gave his blessing," Jacob says. "He says while I'm here, I should tell you about Morgan—about what your mother was like when she lived on the farm."

Hearing her name feels like a gut punch. "Right."

"I was sorry to hear about her passing—I liked her."

"Can we talk about something else?"

"Yeah, sure, any progress on the investigation?" he asks, attempting nonchalance.

My eyes narrow with suspicion as my fingers trace patterns on the countertop. "Jacob, are you worried about how all of this could impact you?"

He hesitates before answering. "I'd be lying if I said I wasn't. I was a part of Sons and Daughters. I'm not completely innocent, as you know. I'm only out right now because I'm still a minor..."

"So that's why you're *really* here? Guilt? To find out what I know?"

Jacob looks at me apprehensively. "It's not just that, though. I like you. I thought we were friends or whatever—"

"I don't have all the answers," I tell him honestly. "But I have faith that everything will work out for you."

"And your dad? How are things fairing for him?"

"Everything's still very much up in the air," I say. "But I can't shake the feeling that Molly's protecting Roger, which is a good thing. The past year has been hard enough."

"Wouldn't surprise me," Jacob concedes, his jaw tightening. "They never found Isaac's body... and with her expertise where the FBI is concerned, it makes sense."

"Listen," I tell him, "if I were you, I'd focus on your own life now. You've got a newfound freedom, and you deserve to enjoy it."

"Easy for you to say," he snaps back, bitterness in his voice. "You didn't have to endure years of psychological torture in that godforsaken cult."

"No," I sigh, my eyes filled with empathy. "But I have my own issues. Besides, you're stronger than you realize. You survived that hell, and you can survive whatever comes next. Just remember, you've got people who care about you."

He nods and forces a smile. "Thanks, Abby."

"Do you ever communicate with any of them? What about Luke?"

"No, most of them are still in jail. Luke's nineteen, and his parents don't have the resources mine do."

He changes the subject. "How are you doing?"

"Haven't been sick yet," I reply with a shrug. "All things considered."

He repeats my words. "All things considered."

I meet his gaze firmly. "I refuse to live my life in fear," I tell him. "I refuse to stay quarantined in that house—not after all of that. I need to keep busy, to keep my mind off everything. I don't know how long I have left, or when my disease is going to flare up—and I want to have experiences, like working my first job."

"Good," Jacob smiles back at me. He points toward the kitchen. "Now go make sure the cook doesn't burn my 'Heart Attack Special,' will you?"

I roll my eyes playfully as I walk away from him toward the kitchen, feeling lighter with each step. The clink of cutlery and low hum of conversation fill the diner and provide a soothing background noise for us both. As I glance around the bustling kitchen, I'm suddenly grateful for this unexpected silver lining.

"Your order's almost up," I say, returning to Jacob.

"Thanks."

"Y'know," I say, leaning in closer to Jacob, "as much as this pandemic has been a nightmare, it's actually given us something we never had before."

He lifts an eyebrow in curiosity. "What's that?"

"Time," I say, running my fingers along the countertop. "Time to reconnect, time for my dad and I to really get to know each other again. And time for me to heal, without the constant pressure of the investigation hanging over my head."

Jacob nods thoughtfully. "The FBI is breathing down my neck, but the pandemic is really slowing things down on that front, so that's good, I guess."

"Yeah, Molly says they're still trying to work it all out."

"They're bringing serious charges against everyone," he says. "It's not the kind of thing that just gets worked out. People are going to prison for a long time—maybe even forever—and that might include me."

"Life's not a straight path, Jacob. It's messy and full of twists and turns. You're young—and now you're here—so maybe let's focus on that."

"You're right," he says. "And it's so good to see you..." He smiles, reaching out to give my hand a reassuring squeeze. "The truth is—I haven't been doing so great on my own, cooped up in my apartment with nothing but Netflix and a rapidly depleting supply of snacks. I was starting to think I might never see an actual real person again."

"God forbid," I tease, rolling my eyes as I pull my hand back and grab a nearby container of wipes. I scrub down the counter. "But, no, seriously, I'm glad to see you too."

Jacob watches me intently. "Is it okay if I just hang for a while?"

I shrug. "So long as you're okay with watching me work..."

"I can help if you want."

I toss him a container of bleach wipes. "We have to sanitize everything like you wouldn't believe. And those are precious, so make them count."

As I'm cleaning, another thought pops into my head, and I can't help but smile.

"Hey, Jacob," I say, smirking at him. "Doesn't the pandemic make you wish we could go back to that cruise ship? You know, just for a little while?" I pause dramatically and add with a sinister grin, "At least there, we never had to worry about running out of toilet paper."

He looks at me and shakes his head. "I'd sooner use sandpaper."

Read the next Britney King thriller: *Ringman* is available on Amazon. Enjoy the first chapter free at the end of this book.

YOUR EXCLUSIVE FREE BOOKS ARE WAITING...
Visit britneyking.com to receive your free starter library. Easy peasy.

A NOTE FROM BRITNEY

Dear Reader,

I hope you enjoyed reading *The Sickness.*

Writing a book is an interesting adventure, it's a bit like inviting people into your brain to rummage around. *Look where my imagination took me. These are the kind of stories I like...*

That feeling is often intense and unforgettable. And mostly, a ton of fun.

With that in mind—thank you again for reading my work. I don't have the backing or the advertising dollars of big publishing, but hopefully I have something better…readers who like the same kind of stories I do. If you are one of them, please share with your friends and consider helping out by doing one (or all) of these quick things:

1. Visit my review page and write a 30 second review (even short ones make a big difference).

(http://britneyking.com/aint-too-proud-to-beg-for-reviews/)

Many readers don't realize what a difference reviews make but they make ALL the difference.

2. Drop me an email and let me know you left a review. This way I can enter you into my monthly drawing for signed paperback copies.

(hello@britneyking.com)

3. Point your psychological thriller loving friends to their free copies of my work. My favorite friends are those who introduce me to books I might like. **(http://www.britneyking.com)**

4. If you'd like to make sure you don't miss anything, to receive an email whenever I release a new title, sign up for my new release newsletter.

(https://britneyking.com/new-release-alerts/)

Thanks for helping, and for reading my work. It means a lot.

Britney King

Austin, Texas

April 2023

ABOUT THE AUTHOR

Britney King lives in Austin, Texas with her husband, children, two very literary dogs, one ridiculous cat, and a partridge in a peach tree.

When she's not wrangling the things mentioned above, she writes psychological, domestic and romantic thrillers set in suburbia.

Without a doubt, she thinks connecting with readers is the best part of this gig. You can find Britney online here:

Email: hello@britneyking.com
Web: https://britneyking.com
Facebook: https://www.facebook.com/BritneyKingAuthor
TikTok: https://www.tiktok.com/@britneyking_
Instagram: https://www.instagram.com/britneyking_/
BookBub: https://www.bookbub.com/authors/britney-king
Goodreads: https://bit.ly/BritneyKingGoodreads
Newsletter: https://britneyking.com/newsletter/

Want to make sure you never miss a release? Sign up for Britney's newsletter: https://britneyking.com/newsletter/

Happy reading.

ACKNOWLEDGMENTS

Many thanks to my family and friends for your support in my creative endeavors.

To the beta team, ARC team, and the bloggers, thank you for making this gig so much fun.

Last, but not least, thank you for reading my work. Thanks for making this dream of mine come true.

I appreciate you.

ALSO BY BRITNEY KING

****For a complete and up-to-date reading list please visit britneyking.com**

Standalone Novels

The Sickness

Ringman

Good and Gone

Mail Order Bride

Fever Dream

The Secretary

Passerby

Kill Me Tomorrow

Savage Row

The Book Doctor

Kill, Sleep, Repeat

Room 553

HER

Around The Bend

Series

The New Hope Series

The Social Affair | Book One

The Replacement Wife | Book Two

Speak of the Devil | Book Three

The New Hope Series Box Set

The Water Series

Water Under The Bridge | Book One

Dead In The Water | Book Two

Come Hell or High Water | Book Three

The Water Series Box Set

The Bedrock Series

Bedrock | Book One

Breaking Bedrock | Book Two

Beyond Bedrock | Book Three

The Bedrock Series Box Set

The With You Series

Somewhere With You | Book One

Anywhere With You | Book Two

The With You Series Box Set

For a complete and up-to-date reading list please visit this page.

GET EXCLUSIVE MATERIAL

Looking for a bit of dark humor, chilling deception and enough suspense to keep you glued to the page? If so, visit britneyking.com to receive your free starter library. Easy peasy.

SNEAK PEEK: RINGMAN

The bestselling author of *HER* and *The Social Affair* returns with a suspenseful tale of crime and passion about a charming sociopath and the criminologist hired to find his killer.

Jason McClure is one of the world's most skilled womanizers. A charming sociopath with a penchant for luxury, Jason is found naked in a dumpster, the only clue to his murder a crumpled photograph stuffed in his mouth.

Camile Brennan is a criminologist hired to consult with the Dallas Police Department on a single task: to find the person—or *persons*—responsible for McClure's death.

Camile, who is equal parts beauty, brains, and narcissist, throws herself into the investigation, which takes a lascivious turn when she discovers photos of multiple women on Jason's laptop, each wearing one of the distinctive rings in the photo from Jason's mouth.

And just like that, she's thrust front and center into Jason McClure's debauched past, which is actually a relief, considering Camile's own life is about to take a rocky turn.

Ringman is a sleek, fast-paced thriller guaranteed to leave even the most seasoned suspense reader breathless.

COPYRIGHT

Hot Banana Press

Cover Design by Britney King LLC

Cover Image by Joe Shields

Copy Editing by Librum Artis

Proofread by Proofreading by the Page

First Edition: 2023

ISBN 13: 9798215029237

ISBN 10: 9798215029

britneyking.com

RINGMAN

BRITNEY KING

"Learn how to see. Realize that everything connects to everything else."

— Leonardo da Vinci

PROLOGUE

He senses it before he sees it. Something's wrong. Matthew Hannah has fifteen minutes until the end of his shift and two hours of work still to do. But he can't think about that now. He needs to check the kennels for blankets and empty the trash bins. Tonight will require at least two trips—the shelter is over capacity.

In the office, another employee is leaving for the day. His coworker heads out the door and down the stairs just as Matthew finishes cleaning the last litter box. He locks the door and jogs to the back of the shelter to grab the trash. Outside, a damp trace of rain is building in the air. It speaks of an imminent storm.

Matthew hurries to load the bags onto a cart. He pushes it through the kennels to the side door, ignoring vicious barks from the shelter dogs. He rolls the cart out into the parking lot, sprinting toward the dumpsters. A chill runs up his spine, and his hair stands on end. Then he looks up—the sky is black, and the orange moon has been snuffed out. Something feels off, and not just the weather. He pricks his ears. Something or *someone* else is here. Matthew takes a deep breath, reminding himself not to panic—the shelter has always been a little creepy at night.

Stillness blankets the city. Streets are deserted because of the weather. An ice storm is coming, but the temperature has already nosedived. He didn't plan to be on the road, but here he is. Something about the best laid plans, he muses, as his cart slams into the dumpster, halting abruptly. Bags of trash spill onto the pavement. One by one, he retrieves them, hoisting the bags over the side of the bin. He doesn't mean to look, but he does. That's when he sees it. The possibility seems so distant. He's sure he's wrong.

There's a foot. *A human foot.*

Surely, it's not real. Matthew is almost certain his coworkers are messing with him. He tosses the rest of the bags in the bin and hauls the cart inside, half-expecting Chris or Ian, and possibly even Sarah, to be standing inside the door waiting to see the look on his face. But they're not. Everyone else has gone home for the day.

Matthew knows what he needs to do, even though he doesn't want to. He can still be wrong. He strides back to the front of the shelter and flips on the floodlights, bathing the entire building in light. It gives him a momentary respite from the panic.

The rest of the trash can wait. Matthew fills food bowls, dishes out medication, and checks that the dogs haven't dragged their blankets into their water bowls. He keeps busy, trying to stay calm. He hopes he's just imagining that foot. But if he's not, he'll have to call the police and risk being stuck at the shelter overnight due to ice. Worse, his record is not exactly squeaky clean, and jail is not an option.

He has to get home. His father is bedridden, and his mother is down with the flu. He hasn't seen her eat in days. She needs a doctor, but Matthew needs his job. He kicks himself for not calling in sick today.

Matthew grabs the remaining trash bags and loads them onto the cart, then takes a flashlight from the office and stuffs it into his jacket. He has to hurry—he's needed at work, but he's needed more at home.

Outside, a low fog has crept its way across the abandoned train tracks. He can't see the lights on the highway anymore; there's just a black void.

He's never liked this part of the city. Lived here his whole life, but the area around the abandoned train tracks has always made him feel uneasy.

The neighborhood is in the midst of being gentrified, but it is still run down. The local churches tried to help the few homeless people who refuse to leave, but some people still feel like they have a home here.

The train tracks are a relic of the local industrial past, long since abandoned. Now it's just a pathway for vagrants and the homeless who refuse to go into the shelters at night. But tonight is different. Tonight they'd freeze to death, and it occurs to him the foot he saw in the dumpster is simply a man seeking shelter. If Matthew leaves him, the elements will kill him, if something else hasn't already.

He calls out and shines his flashlight over the dumpster, pausing where he saw a foot. Something isn't right. He senses danger but can't move.

Then he feels movement behind him and freezes. He doesn't want to turn and see what's there, but he doesn't want to die either.

He whirls around.

There's nothing there.

Shivering, he turns back to the dumpster. He looks down at the pile, shining his light into the depths, and at first he sees nothing.

Then he sees them: two eyes peering from the top of the mound, like two lifeless marbles in a forgotten toy box.

His stomach drops as he stares at the glassy, soulless eyes. Matthew realizes that whatever has happened to this man, he's too late to do anything about it.

What he could not see, nor have predicted, was just how much this discovery was going to irrevocably and inconceivably change the course of his life.

READ MORE: https://books2read.com/ringman

Made in United States
Troutdale, OR
10/30/2023